Cry Wolf, Cry

Russell M. Cera

Outskirts Press, Inc.
Denver, Colorado

Cry Wolf, Cry

V4.0

Outskirts Press, Inc.
http://www.outskirtspress.com

ISBN: 978-1-4327-3666-8

Library of Congress Control Number: 2008941449

PRINTED IN THE UNITED STATES OF AMERICA

Acknowledgements

Foremost, Grace Protano, author of the wittily humorous, delightfully sad memoir *As Long as You Can See the Clock, You're Okay* is my mentor and proofreader. Grace, an excellent writer herself, must receive my deepest appreciation for her indefatigable effort and selfless dedication in editing *Cry Wolf, Cry*. Without her professional guidance, the novel would never have been completed.

Tom Hannon, short story writer and co-author of *Long Island's Easy Writers*, has been a helpful critic of my work, and Lisa Guiloil, author of *The Dragon's Lair*, has also been an inspiration for my having expanded *Cry Wolf, Cry* from its origin as a short story into a full-length novel.

Credit must also be given to my wife Linda for her patience with the numerous rereads of the manuscript. The development of my main characters would not have been complete without Linda's input.

The following people have also contributed either with their encouragement or inspiration: My sons Victor, Gregory and Steven Cera, Andy and Maria Bocchiaro, William Rives, John Piccolo, Kim Brodmerkel, George Johnnidis and Nick Protano.

Finally, Lisa Hendrix from Outskirts Press is recognized for her patience and professional guidance throughout the project.

Preface

In 1926 the last gray wolf in Yellowstone National Park was killed. Before the next decade ended, virtually all wolves in the United States were gone. In less than two centuries, man had succeeded in eradicating two million animals from the North American continent in the most accomplished witch-hunt of the Twentieth Century.

The wolf, enduring the blades of the most cutting media in the world, has been victimized by myths and fables of such magnitude the animal became a symbol of avarice, viciousness and guile. No creature on the planet has been more reviled or more stigmatized. Never has an animal suffered such unthinkable torture or horrifying death. Not ever has a beast generated such fear, nor has one ever been so misunderstood.

Of all the earth's animals, man castigates the wolf more cruelly than any other creature of prey. The wolf, impugned with lies, misconceptions and deceit has been the target of man's paranoia, and has been loathed more deeply for being a predator than any other. It is of wonder that an animal with notions of loyalty, compassion and devotion that appear to be as fully developed as man's should suffer such a consequence.

The first glow upon the dark image of the wolf began with a flicker of hope the animal could be reintroduced to one of its former habitats. In January 1995, fourteen gray wolves were relocated from Alberta, Canada to Yellowstone National Park. That reintroduction stands as the beginning of the Twentieth Century's most prodigious environmental reclamation efforts in the world. Brightened by the glint of a growing understanding and tolerance for the wolf, the project, amidst vehement objection and skepticism, is still underway.

An appreciation of the wolf may evolve by exploring the inner nature of the animal. If we attempt to see the wolf through the eyes of the wolf, to feel its pain, to share its heartache, to experience its joy, to look at its tender loyalty and to know its life, it can be reintroduced not only into the remaining haunts and realms it once enjoyed, but to its greatest adversary in a manner of new understanding. It is an understanding long overdue.

For certain, the persecution of the animal is due largely to the great expanse between mythology and reality. To displace fable with fact, to disprove hundreds of years of misconception is an improbable objective, yet it is the ambition of this work.

In reality, this goal can never be fully achieved. The domain of the wolf has changed, reduced by the chainsaw and the bulldozer. The boundless wilderness that wolves need for survival is gone, irreplaceable. To save the wolf, we must save what remains. No wolves, or for that matter no animal, can be reintroduced to a home that does not exist. But for that which is wild, for those wolves that now survive, and for the men and women who fight to save it all, may this novel be a step in that arduous journey to cross the vast void of misunderstanding.

Prologue

"Wolves have howled at the moon for centuries, yet it is still there."

- Ancient Asian Proverb

When the first germs of life wriggled forth at the dawn of time, so did spirits. As life forms branched into a myriad of organisms, the spirits, each to its own charge, followed. As certain as man arose from those single-celled microbes, gods also evolved with him; and so too did all creatures of Earth inherit their own wraiths.

As the earliest canids developed into the varied species that inhabit our planet, I've grown, changed and developed with them, gradually progressing through the eons to become the spirit of the wolf: an advanced creature, an animal that is superior to all the canids to have ever existed. I am the apparition and the consciousness; I am the embodiment of canis lupus. I am the soul of the gray wolf.

Through the millennia I have been with him. I have stayed close to him, watched him. But I have neither protected nor nurtured him, for the wolf is his own master. Like the other inhabitants of the world, he is on his own to make his way through that infinitesimal stretch of time that is his while he is on Earth. For the time that wolves dwell amongst us, I regard them as being in my charge, not as their keeper, but as their spokesman. All wolves are vocal and are able to communicate, not only amongst themselves, but also to many other inhabitants of our planet. But, because the wolves cannot speak the language of man, I will be their liaison and their voice. I will talk for the gray wolf and I want to tell his story.

From far back in the keep of my youth's memory I have stored countless records of the first canids to appear over thirty-five million years ago. Myriad stories, more plentiful than the stars visible from the darkest forest, are in the archives of my recollect. But there is one more special than the rest. Of all the chronicles, it is the only one I will share with mankind not only because it involves mankind, but also because it is my most cherished tale. It is the story of a wolf family in the modern era, a story about a wolf pack's bold leader I call Bartok and his loyal brother Dakota. It is a tale about the alpha female Shako, her impetuous son Yuma and her omega sister Anoki.

And yet, it is more. It is a story of people, of those who detest wolves and of those who adore them. It is a story of relationships, both human and lupine. It is a story of unthinkable horror and passionate joy, tragedy and valor. It is a tale of boundless love and deep seething hatred, but above all, it is an account of the very nature of my wolves and the essence of their marrow.

CHAPTER 1

"For centuries, wolves have haunted the human imagination. It has been accepted as conventional wisdom that they are savage predators, creatures of nightmare and a never-ending storm of controversy surrounds them."

- Simon & Schuster, Publishers

The full moon had been asleep for hours. Now I saw only Polaris, the North Star, bold and unmoving, challenging the dawn. It blinked before the first rays of the sun, and then faded begrudgingly into the morning light. It was daybreak and Dakota set out to hunt alone, a choice fraught with peril for even the most able of hunting wolves.

The wolves of the pack had not eaten in a week, yet they remained behind. Hunger, like ravenous vermin, gnawed at the walls of their stomachs, but unlike Dakota, they refused to hunt without Bartok, their leader. All eyes fixed on the black wolf as he paced in front of his den like a caged leopard. With each step, the sheen of his silky coat, like inky water on a raven's breast, accented every rippled muscle of the leader's powerful chest. Bartok was preoccupied with something more pressing than hunger, and the pack sensed his concern. The alpha male awaited the birth of pups and his mate Shako was in labor. Shako's sister Anoki and the pack, anxious for the arrival of newborn wolves, would not let her stay alone.

Dakota, too, was reluctant to leave, but another drive from deep within his instinctive genes spurred him to venture out. He was

Bartok's understudy, the beta wolf most loyal to his brother, and the only one that Bartok would allow to share in the responsibility of the pack's survival. Dakota knew the pack would be supportive of Bartok and Shako, but Dakota also knew his presence at the den site was not as necessary as bringing food to the expecting, alpha female. It was more important for her to eat. She had not done so for several days and needed her strength to give birth. Her puppies, more than Dakota, more than any one wolf in the pack, even Bartok himself, would ensure their kind would continue to exist.

The deer that Dakota had been searching for was a victim of the severe winter. It would feed the entire pack if Dakota could locate it. When he drew the odor into his nostrils, Dakota braked in his track. The scent was familiar, but unexpected, and the hackles of his neck stiffened. Now, the sweet smell of venison that he had been following mingled ominously with a noxious smell. Both scents should not have been together, and when Dakota recognized the odor, his legs stiffened like weathered oak, his body petrified, and his tail, as rigid as wood, did not move. Only his head turned as he glanced around.

Once before, Dakota had known the scent when his brother Bartok was with him. The message in Bartok's body language had been enough for Dakota to realize he should avoid the smell.

On that occasion, Dakota was with four other wolves and his young niece Shysie when he heard a new sound whirring in the distance. Bartok reacted, his low growl alarming. Even more frightening to Dakota was to see Bartok cowering in the snow. Little Shysie, confused by Bartok's fear, turned curiously toward the noise, a sound like no other she had ever heard in the wilderness. It was a roar, though with more ferocity than the grizzly's; it was a scream, though more chilling than the puma's; it was a screech, though more piercing than the owl's. Shysie, too, had never seen Bartok react as he did. Her father was always fearless, just as any wolf facing the raging bear. But now, Bartok was whimpering, calling to his daughter to hide from the creatures he knew to be associated with the man-machine.

The noise clanked to a stop and Bartok's whimpers became more urgent. Dakota looked to see Shysie standing at the crest of a knoll, peering in the direction from which the sound had come. He glanced at his brother and knew immediately there was danger for Shysie. Bartok yelped insistently, nagging his daughter to turn back. Shysie ignored the urgency, a deadly mistake. It was an error as lethal as when curiosity disregards the rattle of the venomous snake. When Dakota turned to join in calling to Shysie, horror bolted through his body jolting him back.

An instant before he heard the booming sound, Shysie's fur on the back of her neck exploded with a simultaneous whap, flipping her off of her feet and hurling the little wolf backwards. In the next moment, Shysie lay quivering as her life gushed crimson into the snow. Bartok drew a deep breath and bellowed; his yowling, a mixture of sorrow and anger, shook his brother's core. Dakota had never heard Bartok's voice falter into that staccato tone. Shysie was dead, and Dakota never forgot the sound of his brother's wailing, the mournful moan of a grieving parent for its slain child. Nor would he ever forget the reek of the creatures responsible.

This time when Dakota caught the odious smell mingling with the deer meat, he was within a few yards of the prize. The half-frozen carcass was covered with four inches of new snow, but Dakota's keen nose led him closer. Dakota could tell the faint odor of the feared creatures was not fresh, and he knew they were likely gone. Nevertheless, he swiveled his elegant head, his eyes searching for the absent source. Something in the recesses of his lupine mind began to unfurl, something dark unfolded like a past memory or an old dream telling him to abandon the dead deer that now lay only a few feet away. An older instinct, one from far back in his puppyhood, one that assured life itself, urged him on. The survival of the pack depended upon this instinctive force and he made a decision. Ignoring his fears, Dakota dug into the snow with his forefeet.

A pain so excruciating it nearly knocked him unconscious shot up Dakota's two front legs like shards from a lightning bolt. The spiked jaws of the metal monster crushing his paws, held, and his scream reverberated off canyon walls, echoed down into the valleys, and carried through the great pine forests. The wailing shrieked from the black granite outcrops, resounded into the trees throughout the wilderness back to the wolf pack.

At the den, Bartok jerked his head up from Shako's shoulder. From a great distance away he heard the wails of his brother, shrill and mournful. The entire pack heard Dakota's screaming, but only Bartok would respond.

When Dakota realized he was caught, he yanked backwards and the jawed monster moved with him. For an instant, Dakota thought he was free, until the attached chain reached the end of its slack. When it did, the wolf flipped over and twisted violently, cracking the bones in his forelimbs. Seriously injured, the wolf now realized that he was at war for his life and must fight it the only way he knew how. He clamped his jaws onto the cold steel with such force that he snapped one of his two-inch, canine teeth and badly chipped the other.

Again he cried out, and again he bit down on the relentless hold of the insidious trap. Dakota gnashed at the hardened steel until only one fang and his molars were intact. His voice gurgled in a vibrating wail as blood trickled from his jowls down into his throat.

The excruciation in Dakota's legs slowed time more than the wolf had ever known as he struggled for freedom, twisting and jerking against the metallic demon. The gray wolf moaned again, and then wailed a long, low cry as the pain grew more and more intense. He sat back on his haunches and stared at the demon stabbing spasms of agony into both of his forelegs. Dakota looked over his shoulder in the direction of the den site desperately hoping against the improbable that his brother Bartok might appear. The wolf's ears drooped and his bloody jaw slacked as he glanced back at his woeful predicament. He extended his tongue slowly to lick his paws. As he did, he caught the odious scent of man lingering on the steel jaws that dug deeper into his throbbing forefeet.

The soft, wet tongue yielded no relief to Dakota's pain, so he dragged it over the ice-cold steel as if to offer peace to the tormenting trap. He licked feverishly at the jaws, hoping they might loosen, but he managed only to wash away the ominous scent of humans.

Moments passed in agony and again the wolf glanced toward his home. He thought of his brother back at the den and knew he would not have been in trouble if Bartok had been with him. Bartok was everything to Dakota. He was his leader, his teacher and his spirit.

Dakota's life, as well as the lives of the pack, relied upon Bartok. Without the large, black alpha male, Dakota would not have existed for as long as he had. Without Dakota, Bartok would have a difficult time leading his pack of wolves. Without both wolves, pack survival would be in peril.

Dakota wanted to howl a call to his brother, but he knew that Bartok was tending to Shako and would not stray from her side. There was little hope that Bartok would come to his rescue, but Dakota kept glancing in that direction, nonetheless.

The pain in Dakota's legs turned from piercing spasms to searing heat. As more time passed, the burning spread upward into his shoulders, its fire consuming the nerves throughout the front of the wolf's body. The animal lifted its trapped legs to peer at the iron contraption, and wondered what kind of enemy this jawed monster was that held him in its deathly grip. Now Dakota could no longer feel his front legs and panic overcame him; he knew he was in a war that he could not win. Against his better judgment, he threw back his prideful head, and wailed for his brother.

Bartok heard it all. He glanced at Shako and barked telling her he must leave, though he knew it would be at the worst possible time. To leave Shako now in the throes of labor was abhorrent to him, but to ignore the cries of his brother tested a resolve more deeply embedded into the loyalty of his lupine nature. A loyalty that only a wolf knows for another wolf, an urge to respond, as reliable as the ever-changing phases of the moon. His brother was in need, his lifelong mate, dependent. With overwhelming ambivalence as wavering as the choice between suffering and death, he made his decision.

As he turned to leave the den, Shako yelped to him. She, too, had heard Dakota scream. The alpha female knew the sounds of desperation, fright and pain in another wolf. She understood Bartok's decision, but feared for her mate. She feared for the pack. She feared for herself.

Bartok set out in the direction from which he had heard Dakota's call, his powerful strides spraying snow into the icy air. Barreling through drift after drift, his muscular, prow-like chest defied the frozen, white powder and he tenaciously challenged the expanse between him and his brother.

Dakota lay exhausted in the snow. His legs were numb, and he shivered uncontrollably. Though he was one of the keenest of animals, he knew nothing of the reality that lay ahead. He lived in the moment. Were Dakota to do otherwise, it would not have been fear of dying that made him quake; it would have been the fear of living without his front feet. Had he been caught in the trap by a single paw, he could survive by gnawing through the bone to free his leg and make his way home. Life would be difficult, but with Bartok to help him, he might survive. Having both front paws locked in steel jaws, high on his shins, Dakota would be doomed. No matter how attentive Bartok would be, a two-legged wolf would only be a burden to the pack, jeopardizing its survival. But Dakota's only thoughts were of escape, and his only alternative was to chew through his paws.

Only shards remained of his front teeth. The wolf would have to mouth his legs, one at a time, deeper into his jaws to use his molars to crush the fragile bone. In preparation, he licked his forelegs to soften the skin and separate the fur.

Before starting the gruesome task, Dakota glanced over his shoulder. He saw something. Out of the blackness of despair that darkens the spirit shone a faint light; through the bleakness flickered a glint of hope. For better vantage he forced himself up on his haunches into a position that resembled begging, the trap dangling from extended forefeet as he peered into the distance.

Snow swirled up on the horizon. Something was forging through the blear straight toward Dakota. Through a mist of hot breath and exploding white powder came a bounding, black dot, two hundred yards away. It became bigger and bigger as it neared. At a hundred yards, the dot grew into a figure, and nearer, the figure grew into a wolf.

Bartok!

At full stride, Bartok was fifty yards away when Dakota recognized him. Dakota was saved, if only in his mind.

Before his brother could close the final distance, Dakota squealed a delighted yelp and rolled onto his back, momentarily forgetting his plight. As Bartok arrived, he licked at his brother's muzzle and Dakota shook his entire body in an attempt to wag his tail.

After moments of ritual greeting, Bartok peered at Dakota's

quandary. The pack leader dropped down next to his brother and poked his nose at the trap. Dakota held a steady gaze as Bartok grabbed the steel trap in his jaws to mouth the metal menace. Convinced his teeth were no match for the hardened steel, Bartok licked at Dakota's legs. The two wolves lay side by side for several minutes before Dakota's soft whimpers prodded Bartok. The black wolf rose to his feet and circled Dakota searching for another way to free him.

Dakota never took his eyes from Bartok as though he knew his brother would solve his dilemma. Bartok pawed at the chain and followed it to a ring that was spiked securely into a lodgepole pine stump. Grabbing the chain with his teeth, Bartok yanked. Realizing the ring could not be loosened by a pull, the wolf sniffed at the wood to which it was attached. Testing the stump with his teeth as he had the trap, Bartok began to gnaw at the softer wood.

After a half hour, Bartok's progress slowed. The spikes securing the ring were long and deeply embedded. Gnawing at the wood might take hours. But Bartok sensed that it was his only alternative and continued to bite at the pinewood to gouge out the spikes.

Bartok would stop and rip chunks of meat from the deer carcass and swallow them down. When he was sated, he'd offer venison to Dakota, but the trapped wolf ate none of the proffered meat. Pausing to rest his aching jaws and lick Dakota's face, Bartok was nearly an hour into his chore when he heard the noise. Far in the distance, he recognized the fearful drone.

The two wolves cowered in the snow afraid the sound would come closer, and it did. Within moments, the sound was a roar, and panic shocked through the bodies of both animals stiffening their fur.

The man-machine zigzagged closer and then the noise stopped. Dakota had no choice, but Bartok could escape the frightening figure that climbed from the strange machine and trudged toward them carrying an object similar to the one that killed Shysie. Bartok rose from his crouch. Thickening muscles beneath the flesh of his neck bristled Bartok's ruff as he stood, a snarling barrier in front of his brother. Dakota cowered behind. The buckskin-clad youngster stalked to within ten yards of the wolves, pointing the death stick at one and then at the other.

It was not the first time in the lives of the brothers they had encountered the two-legged beast, and though they had braved animals many times larger, none was so feared as that which approached them. It was the first time either brother ever heard a human voice: “Whoa *shon tonga*. Easy now.”

There was a long pause as the youth looked upon the pitiful sight. One wolf, lowly growling with its eyes fixed in a threatening glare, the other wolf, head drooping with a sullen stare. The boy turned away from the horrific scene and lowered his rifle. Both wolves watched as he dropped to his knees and stared a long, vacant gaze at the quivering wolves, one cowering; one recoiling.

At eye level with the two-legged one, Bartok’s growl softened momentarily, only to resume when the boy got to his feet. “Looks like you lobos got problems.”

The youngster stepped closer for a better look. Bartok snarled loudly and the boy steadied his rifle only on him.

Bartok growled again. He made a mock charge and the boy backed up a few paces. “Ho, now. I not gunta hurt ya. Didn’t mean this to happen.”

The boy backed away, still aiming his rifle at Bartok. Both wolves watched as the boy retreated until Bartok stopped growling. Then, the Indian turned, jogged to his snowmobile and sped off.

A long while passed before Bartok calmed enough to resume gnawing at the wood. He had only gotten a little deeper, when the man-machine returned. Now two of the wolves’ most feared creatures approached, both carrying death sticks. Menace raged from Bartok’s growl; Dakota sidled closer to his brother. Again, Bartok stood, a defiant wall protecting Dakota as one of the creatures pointed his boom-stick at the snarling wolf.

A shot rang out and Bartok yelped. He was hit in the neck, beneath his chin, but did not go down. Furious, he snarled and growled at his attackers, but did not retaliate. Dakota, helpless to do anything, could only whimper and nuzzle against his brother.

The shooter spoke first: “Cayuse, I’m gunna whack him again.”

Waving frantically, the Indian stepped between the man and the wolves. “No! Don’t hurt him more, Mister Joe. Please, no more.”

Moments passed and both people knelt to the ground. The taller man kept a steady aim at Bartok who finally began to calm. When the big wolf became unsteady, a second shot was fired, hitting

Dakota in a flank. The wolf tried to turn to bite at the dart protruding from its hip, but the trap and chain prevented it. Bartok swung around to comfort his yelping brother, lost his balance and fell forward. He tried to get to his feet, wobbled and fell again. Within a short time both wolves succumbed to the tranquilizers and became immobilized, eyes open, but asleep.

* * *

It was late in the day before Bartok began to stir. His body twitched as he tried to push himself up. Within a few minutes, he was able to gain his equilibrium. Within five more, he was steady and on his feet, and the first thing he did was look for Dakota. Bartok whimpered when he realized Dakota was gone. The trap and chain were also gone; the heavy scent of the two-legged beasts was all that remained. Bartok tried to track his brother's spoor, but Dakota's footprints were nowhere to be found, and the only tracks in the snow leading to those of the man machine were from the two-legged ones.

By the time he gave up his search, Bartok was fully alert, but his head drooped low to the ground and his ears flattened from distress. Darkness had fallen and the snow reflected ghostly yellow from a lunar glow. Bartok lifted his head and heaved a long baleful bay. The sound lingered in the icy air before rising to bounce off the full moon and echo back to earth. To Bartok it sounded failure. To Shako and the pack, miles away, it sounded a woeful tone, ringing sadly in their ears, and they answered.

Bartok heard the pack howling. He knew he had to return to it, but the journey back would be the saddest trek the wolf would ever make. After a final glance around, as if wishing his brother to miraculously reappear, Bartok set out for home, carrying with him a burden, like a huge tumor clinging to his heart, heavier than the remains of the deer carcass he towed to his den site. For no matter the wolf's pain, the survival of his pack took over his purpose, and he dragged both loads with the loyal resolve of his lupine nature.

When he arrived, the remainder of the pack, Shako and four new pups would be there. Although his pack helped to lift the wolf's spirits, he would forever mourn the loss of his brother.

Shortly after the tragedy, Bartok moved his band to a new den site. It was his first order of business. He wanted no part of the old territory, jawed metallic monsters, man machines or the scent of the two-legged beasts. Despite the absence of Dakota, the pack flourished. For winter's heavy snows, carrion was abundant, so the alpha wolf and his troupe did not have to hunt much to survive. Still, Bartok remembered his brother and missed him. Hardly a night would pass without Bartok calling to his lost kin with a howl that held a more sorrowful tone since Dakota's disappearance. In a distance, only malevolent wolves heard the call.

CHAPTER 2

"The wolf continues to shoulder a burden shared by no other species on the continent – a harsh unrelenting yoke of human malevolence."

- Gary Ferguson, *Los Angeles Times,* 2008

At a public hearing of the Farm Bureau and the Fish and Wildlife Service in Missoula, Montana, a horde of gruff, angry men clad in an array of camouflage, dungarees and over-worn coveralls, sat listening to a burly rancher. Among the mass, Jeffrey Reese seemed out of place.

Reese, a six-foot tall, clean-shaven, wiry man with the posture of a West Point cadet, wore a neatly pressed denim shirt and creased jeans. His blue eyes, intelligent and penetrating, were fixed on the speaker. He held a notebook in his right hand and jotted notes with his left.

For a moment he wished he were able to follow his boyhood goal. A southpaw with a deadly sinker for the Chicago Cubs would have been ideal, but a torn rotator cuff while pitching for the Northwestern University Wildcats ended his major league dream when he was nineteen. But that was nearly half a lifetime ago. Now, reality seldom held room for fancy.

Reese raked his fingers through thick gray hair. The color was not the salt and pepper gray that comes by age, but a gray more resembling steel. It was as though nature could not make up her mind between the near black tresses of his Mediterranean mother and the cream-blonde locks of his Anglican father.

Tobacco smoke putrefied the windowless room. The stagnant air was so thick with the choking stench that Reese wanted to reach for his handkerchief to filter the pollution, but he fought the temptation. He could feel the sear of glare from disdainful eyes burning into his skin. Using a hanky, he reasoned, would be perceived as a frailty, and he did not want to grant these men any satisfaction. Generally, he didn't care if other people saw his weaknesses, but not so with these men.

Reese knew he had vulnerabilities, plenty of them. Even acquaintances remembered his months of depression and his helplessness in fighting back. Everyone knew of his feeble attempts to flush the misery of his wife's death with drink, but booze only made him sick and sorry. The more he tried to forget by forcing alcohol as his defense, the more defenseless he became, and the remorse only grew worse until he realized the futility and gave up on the liquor. After that, his damages were exposed, his susceptibility evident. His sorrow was a flag of surrender and he waved it for everyone to see.

But these men, who now surrounded him, must not see weakness. These men thrived on the defenseless, fattening on the flesh of the helpless. These men were bullies. Not like the big boy bullies who intimidated smaller boys. These were mean-spirited thugs; these were men who vented their nastiness with hatred.

Reese saw these men as more sinister bullies. They didn't push little boys around to bolster bravado; they didn't shove and punch to accommodate inferior egos. These men, like crusaders of mayhem, were on a different campaign. They carried their wrath to innocent animals to satisfy loathing. They engaged despise so deep that it reached the bowels of Hell itself by wreaking havoc on creatures that cannot fight back. The objectives of their hatred were wolves. These wolf haters wanted to kill them. They wanted to exterminate them, and people like Reese were their enemies.

Thinking about the men surrounding him, Reese could feel a strange connection, yet distantly removed. Like he, these were outdoorsmen; most of them hunted and fished in their leisure time. The wilderness was their milieu, where they found their niches, where they were most comfortable. Like he, they were drawn to nature and the less restricted boundaries of her domain. Reese grew up in rural Illinois not far from the Wisconsin border. The out-of-doors was in his blood as it was in theirs.

But, unlike many of these people who worked out in the open, Reese made his livelihood indoors. The larger portion of his time was spent within the walls of schoolrooms, libraries and office buildings, and he often felt envious of people not so confined. But here jealousy ended. His ordeals were far removed, his ideals vastly dissimilar.

As a writer of the outdoors for *The National Graphic*, Reese found himself at these hearings more often than he liked, listening to one speaker after another give reasons why gray wolves should not benefit from the protection of the federal government.

For an instant, he glanced up at the dense haze that clung to the ceiling like the toxic atmosphere of a foreign world, and then stared back at the podium hoping the burning sensation in his eyes would not make him tear.

Reese felt the discomfort from the metal folding chair bite into the small of his back as he suffered the speaker's claim: "Bush pilots reported seein' dozens o' moose calves layin' dead in the snow, all massacred together. They're the result o' wolves killin' for the sheer joy of it," the man yelled.

Reese waited for the mumbling of disgust to cease before raising his hand. When the chairman recognized him, Reese slowly rose from his seat and turned to face the man who made the last comment. "Excuse me, sir," he said, "but where did you hear that?"

"I said from some bush pilots," came the reply, like fingernails on a slate grating with unmistakable annoyance.

Reese forced meekness in his voice. "Did they take pictures? Did you see proof of it?"

"No! They don't need to take no pitchers. I hearda wolves doin' that before. They kill for the hell of it. Just for fun. We gotta get rid of 'em!"

The crowd roared approval. Shouts rang out as men hissed and groaned; their overly-loud voices slammed into Reese's ears. The noise seemed like men in a crowded pub shouting one above the other to get the attention of the barkeep over the ear-splitting static of a blaring jukebox.

Reese was not a confrontational man, a nature he inherited from his mother, a woman who might disdain a mouse, but do little to harm one raiding her pantry. He sat down as the resound of the gathering slowly quieted to mumbled agreement. Reese fidgeted in the flimsy chair; the discomfort in his spine crept throughout his body. Although outnumbered, again he rose to his feet and spoke up when the murmurings finally subsided.

“That simply doesn’t make any sense.” Disliking the whine of his own voice, Reese drew a deep breath and hardened its tone. “First of all, cow moose go off to have their calves alone. They don’t herd up. Dozens of calves would never be found together dead or alive.”

“We don’t care if it was just two. One dead moose left to rot is one too many.”

“Yeah!” cried out a man speaking directly to Reese. “Damned wolves are wipin’ out the game. They kill everything they can get their stinkin’ teeth into!”

Someone shouted from the back of the room. “Hey, Yankee, did you ever see wolves kill? It ain’t a pretty sight.”

Reese turned looking for the man who spoke out. “Wolves are much smaller than their prey. Their manner of killing is an unenviable task. If that’s a fault, it lies not with the wolf, but within the design of its creator.”

Another man flapped a stubby, weathered hand at Reese gesturing for him to sit down. “We don’t need that fancy talk. Besides, what do you know about it? You from New York? We’re ranchers! Cattle and sheep men.” He glanced at his cohorts, nodded his head and sneered. “We don’t need no city boy telling us ‘bout how to run our business.”

Reese looked around for at least one sympathizer among the horde in agreement against him. “I’m from Illinois,” he said withholding his Chicago address. “I don’t know where you get your information, but I’ve never found that wolves destroy their own ecosystems. There’s only one predator on this planet that kills for the sake of killing.” Jeffrey Reese paused searching the crusty faces of the men eyeing him. He was becoming hoarse from talking, and the choky air contributed to the grinding exasperation in his voice. “And it’s not the wolf!”

Reese felt the futility of his words as he spoke. "Wolves have been here for over a quarter-million years, and for most of that time there were hundreds of thousands more than there are now. If they wiped out their food source for the sheer joy of destroying it, they would never have survived as a species."

An eruption of jeers and boos broke out before the chairman slapped his hand on the dais to bring order back to the room. "The man has a right to his say!" the chairman shouted. "And everything he's said so far is true. Now, unless we conduct ourselves with respect for what others have to say, this hearing will get us nowhere."

For over two hours the opinions of the men were heard. Only a few, but none so vocal as Reese, were against the government's proposal to remove the gray wolf from the endangered species list. Most hoped the wolf could be hunted to extinction.

The meeting over, its stress left Reese slumped forward in the unforgiving chair. With his elbows on his knees he gazed blankly at the notepad in his hands and then closed his eyes to keep out the smoke and listen for the room to empty. As the shuffling sounds of the men scuffling from the auditorium subsided, Reese leaned back, reached a hand around to the nape of his neck to knead at its tenseness, and then opened his eyes. That's when he saw her.

A petite, blonde-haired girl stood staring at him from the front of the room. Surprised that he hadn't noticed her before, Reese turned to scan the huge empty hall wondering where she could have been sitting. When he looked back she had added an alluring smile to her girlish face and began to walk toward him.

Reese rose from his chair as she approached with an extended hand. "Hi. My name's Beth."

Reese held a cool, but firm handshake. "Well, hello there young lady. Just come in?"

"Oh, no. I've been here all evening. Hands are always a little cold."

Usually quick with a response, Reese hesitated trying to figure why a young girl would be at a farm bureau hearing among rough, unkempt men of irascible temperament.

"You're Jeffrey Reese from *The National Graphic*," she said.

"Thanks for reminding me. I was beginning to wonder about that."

"About your identity?"

"About why I'm here."

"You've got a cause."

Suddenly, Reese wondered if he had misjudged her innocence. "I'm sorry. I should have had better manners, but it seems I don't need an introduction."

"The Internet. You can Google anyone who's somebody."

"I'm flattered, but if I wanted to know about you, *Beth* wouldn't work. Only one name?" he asked with a raised brow. "Is that like Fabian or Zeus?"

"Too masculine. Hera, maybe."

"Right. Sorry about Zeus."

"Fabian? Who's that?"

"Another bad reference," he said. "Singer. Teen idol. Way before your time, all face, no voice."

"Well, I can't sing, either, so I'll take it as a compliment."

Like a flower lover to the beauty of a virgin dahlia, Reese's attention was drawn by her face as she spoke, her mouth blooming into a Goldie Hawn smile, beguiling, attractive, enticing him to want more words to follow. "And besides," he said, "Hera was married and I see you're not."

She splayed her left hand and looked down at it. "You noticed?"

"Noticed what?"

"No ring."

"No wrinkles."

Glancing at the thin gold band on Reese's finger, "Wrinkles?" she asked. "They come with marriage?"

"Can't you tell?"

"Not by you," she said.

"A few more meetings like tonight's and I'll have plenty."

She knew Reese was a widower, but did not press about the wedding ring he wore. "I've got more than one," she said.

"Can't be wrinkles. Has to be rings."

"Names. I'm Elizabeth Atkins English. But, please. Call me Beth." Her pleasant face radiated more from the sparkle of her eyes than from the natural color of her rose-pink lips.

"So, Beth, what do you do?"

"I help my father at Elk Woods, our ranch. Cattle business; it's a living."

"Oh, a cowgirl."

"Surprised?"

"Very. And, I won't ask how you know me. Should I know you?"

"Not really. I'm not comfortable being so forward, but I'd like to talk to you for a moment if you have time."

"Time I've got, but if you're looking for an agenda …"

"Agenda?"

"Seems everyone in these parts has a wash list of evils he wants to scrub away by exterminating wolves. Especially the ranchers.

"Honestly, I'm not looking for dirty laundry. Maybe try to clean up a little."

"Pretty quick on the metaphors," Reese nodded, "I'm impressed."

"And without an agenda against wolves," she said.

"No?"

Elizabeth's smile would not wane. "No, Mister Reese; in fact, it's just the opposite. I'd like to talk to you about saving them."

Reese searched the empty room again and then tilted his head as he looked back at the girl who appeared as though she should have been in the company of a chaperone. "Should you be alone at meetings like this?"

"I know. I look like a kid."

"Aren't you?"

"At heart, not age."

"Which is?"

"Should a gentleman ask a woman's age?"

Reese slightly cocked his head. "You assume I'm a gentleman. I assumed you younger than a woman."

Elizabeth took a small step backward and tilted her head just as Reese had. "Aren't you a gentleman?"

"Aren't you younger than a woman?"

"How about a young lady?" she said.

"You're getting a little picky. I guess you're a woman after all, and in that case I'd never ask."

Elizabeth laughed, "Care to guess?"

"Not a chance. That's more dangerous than asking."

"Okay. A young lady it is, but take a guess. I can use the flattery."

"Don't insist."

"I insist."

"You're a woman all right." Reese stepped back, touched his chin with his index finger and glanced at her as if to judge a contestant in a pageant. "Let's see. I'd say -- Eighteen," he announced forcing conviction with a scrunched brow.

"Not bad, you only missed by a decade."

"Gee. You don't look a day under eight."

"You're funny."

"Twenty-eight? No. Looks more like eighteen to me."

"And you lie," she said wrinkling her nose.

Reese was surprised. The sweetness of her face and small stature made her appear much younger. "Look, I'm sure you can take care of yourself, but this is a rough crowd. You seem a little out of your element here for someone who's going to disagree with the consensus."

"These people don't know my opinion. They think it's like my dad's. Most of these men know me through him and that's enough to discourage them from bothering me."

"Daddy sounds tough. What's his name?"

"He's not so tough, but I guess the name's intimidating to some. John Dalton English is my father. Ever hear of him?"

Reese thought he had heard the name connected with negative activity towards wolves. "Name's familiar, but I've never met him."

"People call him J D. I came here for him. He had other business."

Reese bristled. He felt as though he had let his guard down. "Let me guess. Anti-wolf rally? Den raid?"

As though preparing a prolonged explanation, Elizabeth took a deep gulp of air, but exhaled slowly as she changed her mind. "Really, he's not well enough to travel too much these days, but let's just say he wouldn't have agreed with you."

"Which part? What I said about the wolves not killing for fun?"

"No. He's not stupid. Quite the opposite," she said, her smile beginning to fade. "He's a business man and protected wolves are not good for business."

Reese smirked. "Unprotected, there'd be no wolves. Is that what you people want?"

"Not all of us."

"I sure didn't hear anyone say that tonight."

"I just couldn't speak out."

Reese turned to walk away. Her smile nearly gone, Elizabeth grabbed at his sleeve. "Mister Reese, you don't understand. I know you think ranchmen want that. Maybe they do. Maybe even my father wants that. But it seems to me there are some of us who might want something better for wolves. Don't you think?"

Reese was still unsure of the girl's intentions. He spoke to her slowly, his tone icy. "A voice of reason from the enemy's daughter? What would daddy think?"

Elizabeth shuddered. Lashes, brushy thick despite the absence of mascara, swept over hazel eyes. As if in a confessional, she lowered her head and spoke. "Mister Reese, that's what I wanted to talk to you about. I don't agree with my father, but he is my father. I know how he feels. I'm afraid of the things he says he'll do. I don't want to see the wolves killed. Honestly, Mister Reese, I want you to believe that."

Reese sensed genuine discomfort and he softened his voice. "I guess you never read 'Little Red Riding Hood,' did you?"

"Yes, and the 'Three Little Pigs,' but I still don't hate wolves, Mister Reese."

Reese's face pursed into a grin. "Call me Jeff. Okay?"

The lights flashed in the room. A man nearly as thin as the push broom he was leaning on called out: "Time's up folks. Gotta sweep."

Reese waved a hand and nodded to the custodian, turned and escorted Elizabeth into a cluttered foyer. Posters, bulletins and notices festooned the corkboard walls of the small anteroom where he helped her into her blue peacoat. "I'd have expected you to be wearing fur," he said with a half-smile.

"I'm not what you think, Jeff. I'm not against what you would like to see for those animals."

Elizabeth's eyes bored into Reese's until he lowered his stare and spoke to the dimple of her chin. "I don't know what to think. You know my name. You know what I do, and seem interested to find out more. Your father is an opponent of wolves, sends you here and you say you disagree with him. What should I believe?" Reese asked with a shrug as he raised his eyes again to meet hers.

"It's true. He did want me to come, but he has no idea that I wanted to meet you."

"So you're here to meet me and he thinks …"

Elizabeth interrupted, "He's heard you speak before and he's talked about you. That's how I knew your name." An upturned wrinkle crept back across her lips and she winked. "The rest I found out for myself."

Reese warmed more. "Google's great. Isn't it?"

A broader smile flooded the girl's face and its glow pleased Reese. "Yes," she said heedlessly pulling a flyer from its pushpin off a cork bulletin board and extending it to him. "Would you write down your number? I promise not to be a pest, but I'd really like to talk more."

To her surprise, Reese rejected the flyer. "Why not?" he said as he tore a page from his notepad to jot his phone number on. "It's been a long time since an attractive woman asked for my phone number."

As Reese was writing, Elizabeth glanced at the flyer she had pulled from the wall and looked with more interest at its bold print: STOP THE MENACE. A picture below the headline was of a snarling, red-eyed wolf foaming at the mouth. Elizabeth flushed when she looked up to see Reese watching her.

"Not his best side," he said smiling at her reaction.

"Jeff, I agree with you. It's difficult for me. My father's a good man. He's caught up in this de-listing thing with all the other cattlemen. Please try to understand."

Reese shook his head. "It's late, Elizabeth. Be safe going home. Call me whenever you'd like."

CHAPTER 3

"This is the measure of wolves as a species: to be born, to struggle to survive, feel pain, express joy, and eventually die."
- Scott Ian Barry, *Wolf Empire*

After he walked Elizabeth to her green Chevy Blazer, Reese trudged to his Jeep Cherokee, struggled in and forced the seat back more than usual so he could stretch his long legs to relieve the tightness. It was cold and beginning to snow, but he did not turn on the heater. Instead, he zipped up his tan, goose-down parka and enjoyed its warmth. He loved the softness of the puffy coat. It brought back memories of his wife Samantha. She had given him the parka as a birthday gift nearly seven years before, and Reese knew his favorite coat could defy any chill.

The farther Reese got from the civic center, the more he could feel the tenseness leave his body. "Some way to spend an evening," he said aloud. "Arguing with these people is futile. I just don't understand how they can be so wrong about those animals."

Transfixed with the snowflakes dancing in the beams of his headlights, Reese stared into the night on the lengthy drive to his cabin. Like the faint heat of tiny candles transforming their wax, the warmth of the parka melted into his skin and his thoughts began to drift. Samantha was on his mind. She would have understood. She would have sympathized about the plight of the wolves. She would have cringed to hear of the vehemence against them. She would have wept if he told her of the slaughter, the torture, the baited fishhooks to drag pups from their dens and the intentional infliction of deadly sarcoptic mange that spread throughout an entire pack painfully eating away at the wolves' skin. She would have comforted him when he anguished about how his work on the wolf project was breaking his spirit.

He thought about his dog Gretchen and spoke to the snowflakes pelting the windshield. "How can so many people disdain the wolf and yet love their dogs? I just don't see that much difference between the two. Sammy would have loved my Gretchen."

For nearly five years before Gretchen came into his life, Reese hated to return home after he had been away for a while. The same mind war would rage in his head, the vicious fight between grief and guilt, punching and kicking. The grief that he felt for the loss of his young bride Samantha punched at his heart like an iron fist; the guilt that he bore for not being home in her time of need kicked at his gut like an enraged mule. His grief felt more piercing than any implement of torture and the emptiness of a one-bedroom flat after Sammy's death was intolerable. Reese, on his way home, would often force himself to dally as much as possible, like the last drunk to leave an open-bar party.

Now, the return was more bearable. Spinning and yipping, Gretchen's greetings were the embodiment of exuberance and Reese could not stay away from the dog any longer than necessary. As he pulled up the long, twisting, blue-cindered driveway and neared the log-frame bungalow, Reese could see his dog propped up to a window, head wagging from side to side, keeping cadence with a frenzied tail. Despite the isolation he felt after the meeting, Jeff Reese was glad to be back to the cabin he had been living in since arriving in Stevensville.

When Reese opened the door, Gretchen could hardly contain herself, squealing and shaking her whole body to flag her greeting. He kneeled by the dog as she tumbled to her back to get the belly rub she had been waiting for.

"How's my girl? Miss me, did ya?" Reese laughed. "C'mon Gretch, let's take a walk before we hit the sack."

Reese spent the next half hour playing with Gretchen in the fresh snow. He was tired and wanted to go to bed more than anything, but he couldn't disappoint the dog. He knew she looked forward to her nightly jaunt and he forced himself to please her.

The next morning, Reese nursed a steaming cup of black coffee while opening his mail. The German shepherd curled at his feet had been his only companion for the past seven weeks that he had worked on the wolf project.

"Damn it, Gretch. This guy just doesn't get it!"

Gretchen looked up and cocked her head. Alone in the fire-warmed cabin, the dog knew Reese was talking to her. Sitting up, the shepherd's ears cocked forward. She stared at the man who barked cranky words as though his dog understood.

"Sometimes I wonder how these editors get their jobs. I write to this guy because he prints an article that makes the wolf seem as if it's a man-eater, and all he can do is respond that the animal is not endangered. Damn! It's on the list," he shouted.

Sensing her master's disquiet, the dog shoved a paw at his knee. Reese knew the dog was sensitive to his mood and he reached to stroke the side of her jet-black muzzle.

For the dog's sake, he altered his tone. "I'm not angry at you, girl. I'm miffed at Thornberry 'cause he hates wolves. You know what I think, Miss Gretchen? He'd probably even dislike you. Now how could anybody not love you?"

He reached down and rubbed the back of the dog's ears. Gretchen rolled her eyes back and nudged her nose toward his face. She loved the brisk ear rub more than any other display of affection.

As soon as Reese stopped petting, the dog stood up and glanced toward the door. "I get the message. Now you want to go out, don't you, Gretch?"

Reese shook his head. "How do you know I don't have to work today? But somehow you know, right? I wish I could figure that out. I pay more attention to you than I do to my job, but it's never enough, is it?"

Gretchen wriggled and barked and Reese laughed. "That's right, demand more of my time."

Reese knew that she hated those hours he had to be afield. Whenever he made preparations to leave for work, Gretchen would sulk. If he were going to dedicate time to her, she seemed to tell the difference and her jaunty shuffle and spin antics were unmistakable.

"Okay. Okay. C'mon Gretch. Let's go for a walk and forget about old Thornberry for a while. I'll get back to that --- that guy some other time."

The dog dashed for the cabin door spinning merrily and yipping as Reese reached for his parka when the phone rang.

"Hello."

A raspy voice that Reese didn't recognize rattled from the receiver. It was a hollow voice, inarticulate and grating to his ear. "Hello, my name's Joe. Is dis Reese?"

"Yessir, it is. How may I help you?"

"Ya know Charley Whittington, the conservation guy? Well, he told me you might be interested in somethin' I got."

"Yeah, I know Charley. What is it that you have?"

"A wolf. A gray wolf."

"A wolf? Is it alive? Where is it?"

"Yeah, he's hurt kinda bad, but even though Doctor Ferris ain't no vet, he thinks he can fix 'im up."

"Are you sure it's a wolf?"

"Oh, it's a wolf awright, a big male. An Indian kid caught him in a trap. Says he was trying to catch a wolverine or somethin', and caught the wolf by mistake."

Stunned momentarily, Jeff Reese was silent.

"Mister Reese?"

"Yeah. Yeah, I'm here. Sorry. Where is it now?"

"That's a problem. Right now he's over at Doc's place, but he can't stay there. Charley says you're writin' stories 'bout wolves and you might be able to help me."

"Joe, I'm sorry. What did you say your last name was again?"

"Last name's Morton. I been livin' in Montana my whole life and I ain't never seen no wolf 'round here before. Never knew they were so damned big! Gotta be way over a hundred pounds."

"Mister Morton, I'm a journalist. I'm doing a series of articles on wolves in the Bitterroot area for a national magazine. How can I help you?"

"Charley says you're staying here in Stevensville and you might keep the wolf a few weeks until it heals up enough to let 'im go."

Sitting near the door, Gretchen whimpered softly, got to her feet and circled several times before sitting again to paw at the door and glance back toward Reese. Reese called her to his side and she obediently sat down at his feet as he turned his attention back to the phone.

"This is the best news I've heard since I've been in Montana. Where did you say the kid caught it?"

"He was trapping up a ways from Bass Creek. Dumb Indian calls me yesterday. He's only a kid, maybe fifteen, sixteen. Says he needs my help. I go up there with 'im and here's this wolf in a jump trap an' another one tryin' to protect it."

Reese's mouth hung open for an instant before the words came out. "There were two wolves?"

"Yeah. I had to dart 'em both. The other one was even bigger. Real big, black one. I'd guess he'd go about 140 pounds, maybe more."

"I knew wolves were reported to be living on the benches above Bitterroot Valley. I guess these were from that pack. Did either have collars or tags?"

"No, nuthin."

"Wow! Then they're not from the Big Hole or the Kelly Creek packs. Must have come over from the Idaho border," Reese said, talking more to himself than to Morton.

"So, Mister Reese, do ya think you kin keep the thing at your place for a spell? He looks kinda calm."

Reese switched the phone from one ear to the other as he thought about the question. "I don't know. It'd be an experience, but it seems like a bigger deal than I could handle. Did Charles say it would be okay without a permit?"

"He didn't say nuthin' about no permit or anything."

"I don't want trouble with the Conservation Department. My magazine won't pay if I get fined," Reese said with a slight laugh.

"He said you'd prob'ly get more flack from ranchers than from his guys. But he says that your place is kinda far away from town, so no one will know you have 'im."

"Is he crated?"

"Biggest cage we could find. It'll hold a grizzly, but Whittington says the conservation guys will build a fence for 'im if you agree."

"Sure. I guess. Like I said; it'll be an experience. Bring him over."

Turning to his dog as he hung up the phone, Reese was ecstatic. "Did you hear that Gretchen. We're going to have company!"

The shepherd yipped when she recognized the excitement in Reese's voice. "We're going to have a relative of yours staying with us for a while."

Gretchen barked, spun around and wagged her tail as Reese put on his parka.

* * *

The next evening, Charles Whittington, along with Doctor Andrew Ferris and Joe Morton arrived with the rare cargo. The three men hoisted the crate from the pickup truck and placed it on the ground in front of Reese. Reese kneeled on one knee to look into the cage and felt the strength leak out of his heart and clog into the pit of his stomach.

One of the most handsome specimens of canis-lupus looked more pathetic than any other Reese had ever seen. Crammed as far back as it could get into the horrific cage cowered a pitiful-looking creature, tail tucked tightly between the hind legs of its sagging back, head drooping, and totally stripped of its once-proud spirit. A large cone collar around its neck and soft-casts on both of its forefeet, the animal whimpered its plight.

"Do you know how the dictionary defines gray wolf?" Reese asked rhetorically. " 'Dog-like and savage.' Of course it's dog-like, but there's nothing remotely savage about this guy," Reese groaned as he stared at the bewildered animal cringing in fear.

Reese rose from his knee and looked at the men staring at him as they digested his reaction. Except for Morton, sad expressions darkened the faces of the silent men.

Morton grinned, "I think that wolf's a goner."

Charles Whittington, a tall willowy man whose repute for being one who would act on a matter rather than talk about it, tilted his head raising one brow above the other with a glance at Morton. "Now we don't know that, do we Joe?" he said as he arched both brows and stared until Morton looked away.

Whittington stood with his arms folded across his narrow chest glaring at Morton. "Listen, Jeff," he said with the slightest hint of a

French-Canadian accent that seemed to slip words through a thick mustache in a way barely making it possible to see his lips move. "You don't have to do this if you don't want to."

Reese lifted his left hand over his shoulder to cup the nape of his neck and tilted his head back as he spoke. "I must be nuts to do this, Charley."

Whittington searched Reese's face, shrugged and then gently shook his head. "Whatever you want to do, Jeff. I know this won't be easy, but unless you take him I'm afraid we may have to put him down."

"That's not even an option," Reese said turning to Doctor Ferris. "Doc, what do you say?"

Ferris gave a reassuring wink. "I think the animal has a good chance to recover. Except for his teeth, he looks a lot worse than he is. His legs are fractured, but there's no bone separation and they should knit back pretty fast. He's on heavy antibiotics 'cause the trap cut him up some, but otherwise he should be good as new in a month or so."

Reese was still wondering if he did the right thing in agreeing to keep the wolf. "What'll I feed him?"

Morton snickered. "Alpo. Purina Wolf Chow. What do you feed your dog?"

Again Whittington glowered at Morton before answering Reese. "Raw meat, road kill, anything it will eat in the wild. But don't worry about that. We'll bring you all you need."

Thinking about the other wolf, Reese turned to Morton who stood wide-eyed as if waiting to fling into the conversation. "Was the one that was with this guy hurt, too?" Reese asked.

"Oh, no, no," Morton blurted, eager to contribute some information. "He seemed okay, but really mad. He was trying to chew the trap's chain off a stump to free this one here. Almost got it off, too."

Whittington stroked his black mustache with the tips of his fingers and sighed. "It's a good thing he didn't," he said as he refolded his arms across his chest. "This guy would have died with that trap hanging on him like that. His teeth are broken, but between him and the pack, they'd a chewed that trap away, paws 'n' all."

Reese shook his head. "What a horrible thought. I don't even want to think about it."

But he did think about it. The wolf was the only thing he could think about for the next four days as a crew from the forest service built a huge holding pen. He tried to offer the animal food, but it refused everything but water. Although apprehensive about opening its cage, Reese discovered the wolf made no attempt to snarl or snap at him when he did. Reese could only imagine the hell the animal must have endured. He would be happy when the enclosure was finished. At least then, the wolf would not shiver in fear of being encaged in a wire crate.

CHAPTER 4

"Wolves housed in cages are among the most pitiful of all caged animals."

- Konrad Lorenz, *King Solomon's Ring*

Dakota was trapped again, and the smell of the two-legged creatures was everywhere. There was something around his neck that stuck out beyond his muzzle that would not allow him to tear away the detestable bindings on his legs. He made repeated attempts to push against the confining sides of the frightening box he was in, and the nails of his exposed paws were cracked and torn from his constant scratching at the opening of the cage.

Whenever a two-legged one would come near, Dakota's terror gripped tightly, squeezing the muscles of his bladder until it lost control. He was constantly twisting his head like a mad cow to fight the hideous collar. Feeling had returned to his paws, but it was painful for him to stand for any length of time, so he stayed on his belly, far back in the dark of the crate.

When the eight-foot-high chain-link enclosure was completed, Reese watched as the wolf was brought into the quarter acre fenced pen and the restraining-cage opened. As soon as the men were far enough away, the animal made a painful effort to burst from the cage. With the cone collar and soft-casts hampering it, the wolf scrambled from confinement, but Reese thought the sweet taste of freedom the animal must have felt, soon dissipated when it reached the fence of the enclosure. He had empathy for the wolf. He imagined that it must have realized yet another obstacle between it and the life to which it so desperately wanted to return. Reese cringed as the wolf made several feeble dashes along the pen's perimeter, and one desperate leap like a crippled rabbit trying to escape its warren. Weakened, Reese saw the famished soul finally collapse in exhaustion at the back end of the enclosure as far from the restraining-cage as it could get.

For the next few days Reese saw the wolf circle the enclosure, searching for a way out. It made pathetic efforts to paw the fence and the earth beneath it, but its bandaged forelegs afforded no purchase, and it finally stopped trying. The animal's instincts told it that its den and pack lay to the west as it examined the steel fence in that direction, nudging and pushing at it in vain. After a few days, the defeated wolf began to give up his life. Refusing any food from the offensive smelling humans, the animal looked weak and miserable. This refusal to eat had Jeffrey Reese worried and he could hardly sleep.

* * *

It was nearly midday when the phone awakened Reese from a much-needed nap, but he answered it with his customary pleasant tone. "Hello, it's Jeff."

"Hello Jeff, It's Beth English. Remember me?"

Reese was surprised to hear her voice, but even more surprised at the flow of warmth he felt pulse into his chest at the sound of it. "Yes, I remember you. You're the woman who looks like a kid."

"What an impression," she said.

"There's more."

"I hope so."

"You're the pretty girl with the perpetual smile."

"That's more like it. And, very original."

"Original?"

"Yes. I've never heard that one before."

"Sounds like you think it's a line."

"No," Elizabeth assured. "Just original."

"Good. I stopped using lines years ago."

"Why?"

"They never worked."

"I think you're fibbing again."

"No, honest. I was lousy at it, besides, how could anyone not notice that you form every word with a smile? I don't know too many people who speak and smile at the same time. I like it."

"Well, thank you."

"And how could I have forgotten someone from this neck of the woods who claims to be pro wolf?"

"I really am, you know."

"I think you made that clear, but now I can test you," Reese said.

"Really? How so?"

"I'll introduce you to one. Have you ever had the pleasure of making a wolf's acquaintance?"

"Nnnno. Can't say that I have. Have you?"

"As a matter of fact I have. I have one as a house guest," he said.

"You're joking. You have a real wolf?"

"I'm nursing a hurt one back to health. Or at least I'm trying to."

"Do you think I can come see it? Please. I'd love to see it. Please."

Suddenly Reese wondered if he had done the right thing to mention having the wolf to the daughter of a man who wanted them eradicated.

"I'm way up in the sticks. It wouldn't be easy to get here," he said hoping to discourage her.

"You're staying in Stevensville; I'm just outside of Alberton, not that far away. Thirty-five, forty miles or so."

Reese was still a little skeptical. "Right. The Internet. You probably don't even need directions."

"Only a few," she laughed. "How about tomorrow around noon. Please. I'll bring lunch if you'll say yes."

"Heart through the stomach, huh?"

"Whatever works. I really want to see the wolf. Please!"

"I don't know. I never could resist a meal."

Reese reluctantly made the date, gave Elizabeth directions to the cabin and immediately began to have regrets. For the rest of the day he tried to preoccupy himself with Gretchen. He talked to her as though she were his conscience. If no other people were around, the dog sat up and watched Reese's every move whenever he spoke at length. Reese knew that she was waiting for a single word she might recognize, but he pretended to himself that she was deeply engrossed in everything he had to say.

"Gretch. You've been my only girl for years. I don't even know what to say to a woman. Now I have one coming for a picnic."

Gretchen cocked her head and Reese continued. "Now, when she gets here tomorrow, you'll have to be my buffer. Okay? Between you and that old wolf I should be able to entertain her for an hour or so before we throw her out."

Gretchen yipped at the last word and charged for the door. Reese chuckled. "You've got a single track mind. You know that?"

* * *

It was shortly after noon the next day when Elizabeth arrived. As Reese went out to greet her, she lifted a wicker lunch box from the back hatch of her SUV.

Reese glanced at the young woman. It had been a long time since he had taken interest in the appeal of the opposite sex. Though dressed in blue jeans and a denim shirt, she appeared less boyish than he remembered. The sun gave highlights to her gold hair and radiance to her fair skin while the cling of her denims revealed the delicate contours of a nicely proportioned woman.

The slight turn of Elizabeth's head didn't hide a wide grin. Reese could feel the flush of warmth tingle into his skin as he realized he had been caught in a stare. The best way to react, he thought, was to be truthful. "You sure are a pretty girl," he said. "I can't seem to be cool about noticing good looks."

"Well, I'm not convinced," she said, "I think you have a very cool way of telling a woman she's attractive."

"I'm sure I didn't let you in on a secret."

"And I'm sure glad you didn't try to keep it a secret."

Reese breathed a soundless laugh and changed the subject as he reached for the wicker box. "Here, let me help you with that. What's in the basket?"

"Hope you're hungry; I made a few sandwiches. You like chicken?"

"Love chicken and I'm always hungry," Reese said.

After Reese took the basket, Elizabeth patted her flat stomach. "Me, too."

"Sure doesn't look to me like you eat very much."

"Ah, but I do, and I like people who like to eat as much as I do."

"Then I guess you're going to really like me."

Elizabeth flashed her brilliant smile. "When can I see the wolf?" she asked glancing around the property and then back at Reese.

"Ah, ha! You're looking at him, little Miss Red Riding Hood."

Elizabeth laughed. "You don't look so big and bad to me."

"Damn. I never could pull that off."

"Sorry 'bout that."

"How about a coyote? Wily enough?" Reese said turning to offer a profile.

Elizabeth tilted her head. "Hmm, no. Fox. Yes. Definitely a fox."

"I'll take it. Come. The real thing is around back," he said as he led Elizabeth to the enclosure.

When she saw the wolf, she could not contain her delight. "Wow, he's huge! I had no idea they were so big."

"Their long legs make them tall, but he's bigger than any wolf I've ever seen. He's probably thirty inches or more to the top of his shoulders."

"I can't believe how beautiful he is. Will he be okay?"

"If I can get him to eat, he should recover, but so far I haven't had much luck with that."

"Can we go closer to the fence," she asked reaching for Reese's hand.

Reese led her to the enclosure. Holding onto the warmth of Reese's palm with her right hand, Elizabeth touched the coolness of the fence with the fingers of her left. "Seems a pity to see him in a pen," she said softly.

The wolf cowering in the far corner of the enclosure held a steady glare. Reese looked over at the wolf and could see its eyes fixed on his. He felt the unmistakable stare of distrust that seemed intended for only him. "To put a wild wolf in a cage," Reese said, "is just not right."

By herself in silence, Elizabeth stood watching the animal as it now paced to and fro along the back of the fence. Reese left her alone to set up a small table on the back porch of the cabin. It was

Elizabeth's suggestion they eat lunch where she could watch the wolf. When Reese returned, the wolf stopped pacing and again resumed its glare.

"He watches you like a hawk," Elizabeth said.

"He knows I enter the pen. He's worried that I will again."

"Aren't you afraid when you go in?"

"Not at all. I just wish he wasn't afraid of me."

Reese coaxed Elizabeth away from the pen, and she reluctantly walked with him to the porch glancing back at the wolf as she followed.

Before they sat down, Reese gave Elizabeth a serious glance. "I have a girl friend I'd like you to meet. Do you mind if she joins us?"

Elizabeth's smile vanished in surprise. "Is she here?"

"Tied up inside."

"Tied up?"

"Jealous type. You know how they can be."

Elizabeth raised one brow in a suspicious arc. "Then maybe you should keep her tied."

"I'll let you meet her, then you can decide," Reese said as he went into the cabin and brought Gretchen outside.

When she saw the German shepherd, Elizabeth's laughing reaction assured that she liked dogs, and Reese made the introduction. "This is Miss Gretchen. She's my best girl."

The dog wriggled over to Elizabeth and made an instant friend. "Jeff, your dog is a sweetie. She's one of the prettiest shepherds I've ever seen."

"I guess I'm just a sucker for attractive girls."

Reese's wink made Elizabeth grin. "I can't get over how friendly she is. Is that usual for her breed to take to strangers like she does?"

"Smelling like a chicken sandwich doesn't hurt."

Elizabeth broke into a laugh. "I washed my hands after making them."

"The nose knows. You just can't hide the smell of a chicken sandwich beneath a little soap and water."

Reese didn't want the dog to disturb the wolf, so he tethered Gretchen to the porch close to Elizabeth while they ate. Reese enjoyed the woman's company, surprised at how easy it was to talk to her.

Elizabeth kept glancing at the pen. “Tell me about the wolf.”

“There’s not much to tell. He was trapped. A boy caught him by mistake and the conservation department thought he might be safe here until he heals.”

“Safe from cattlemen?” she asked, her voice soft and as shy as a confession from a guilty child.

Reese recognized her discomfort. “Not all of them. Some like wolves,” he said with a wink and a grin.

Elizabeth smiled back.

The more they talked, the more comfortable Reese felt about opening up to Elizabeth. Her interest in the plight of the gray wolf seemed genuine, and any suspicions Reese may have had about her loyalty to her father’s cause began to diminish as she spoke of the atrocities she overheard when her father had other ranchers to his home.

“When we met, you used the term ‘den raid.’ I knew what that was,” Elizabeth confessed. “I couldn’t believe men could be so cruel to smoke puppies out of their dens and club them to death. You really have to hate to do something like that.”

She looked at Reese shaking his head, her voice softening to a whisper. “Where did that hatred come from?”

Reese knew of more horrific accounts, but he chose not to go into detail. “Fear,” Reese said. “Fear of the unknown, I guess.”

“My father says wolves are fiends. Is he wrong about all of those stories? Is he wrong about wolves hunting and killing people?”

“Yes. He’s wrong. It’s not his fault; he’s been misinformed. And that misinformation has been passed to people from generation to generation.”

Reese leaned back in his chair. “You see, Beth, the wolf is a unique creature, possibly one of the most adaptable animals on the planet. The wolf we know today is not the same as the one our ancestors knew. People came to this country with preconceived fears and hatred. Some of it was based on fact, I’m afraid, but most is just not true.”

Elizabeth begged to hear more. “I know the Indians lived peacefully around wolves before white men ever set foot on this continent,” she said, “but why is it that people who probably never even saw a wolf could not settle amongst them?”

"I think if we knew more about what those people believed when they came here, we'd understand. Compared to the vast wilderness wolves had on this continent, most European countries did not have that kind of space. There, wolves and people lived closer to one another."

Absorbed, Elizabeth leaned forward. Reese noticed and continued. "Early history tells us that Europe was a progression of one bloody war after another. As those conflicts grew, so did the number of dead left behind."

Reese gazed toward the enclosure. "The Hundred Year's War alone left thousands of human corpses strewn on the battlefields. Wolves are opportunists," he shrugged. "With their habitat destroyed from the wars and their natural prey depleted to levels unable to sustain them, some wolves turned to scavenge those dead. People witnessed this, and, as you can imagine, it must have horrified them beyond belief."

Elizabeth shook her head and reached down to stroke Gretchen's back as Reese spoke: "Frightening accounts turned into exaggerated stories. And the exaggerations grew worse."

Stirring in his chair, Reese spoke as if he found his own words difficult to believe. "Some wolf packs developed a preference for human flesh and came into villages and towns. From what I know of today's wolves, it's hard to imagine, but records say that in the 1400's wolves attacked and killed people right in the city of Paris."

Looking at Elizabeth, he said: "Did you know that the Louvre got its name because it was built where wolves were frequently seen."

"No, I didn't know that."

"Yeah. It's believed the original structure was built as a lodge for wolf hunts. Louvre comes from the Latin words lupus or lupara, meaning wolf."

Elizabeth gazed at the wolf pacing the fence-line. "That's so interesting," she said. "No wonder people think the way they do."

"I wish people didn't think that way, but I'm afraid it's a legacy the animal is never going to escape. Heck, in the Middle Ages the Catholic Church even went so far as to declare the wolf 'the devil's dog,' proof of Satan walking the earth," Reese said as he, too, stared out at the restless wolf.

The rest of the day passed as easily as the conversation. The more they talked, the more Reese realized how torn Elizabeth was about her father's position as an activist to eliminate wolves.

It was much later than she had planned to stay when Elizabeth finally decided to leave. Reese and she went over to the enclosure once again so they could take another look at the wolf that finally had settled down to rest. As soon as Reese neared the fence, the wolf jerked to its feet. Its attention to Reese was as suspicious as any captive to a jailer.

"Maybe I shouldn't get too close," Elizabeth said.

"I don't think it's you he's concerned about."

"Sooner or later I think he'll realize you're trying to help him."

"Well, if I can't get him to eat pretty soon…." Reese stopped as if he was afraid to finish his thought. "Come on," he said, his voice changing to a more cheerful tone, "I'll grab your lunch basket and walk with you."

"Thanks for inviting me out," she said. "I'm glad I met Gretchen and the wolf. I had a great day."

"Me, too," Reese said. "Me, too."

"May I call you again sometime, Jeff?"

"Sure. I can't resist chicken sandwiches," Reese said with a wink as he handed her the empty lunch box.

Elizabeth laughed and kneeled down to give Gretchen a final petting before saying goodbye. Reese watched as she backed down the long and narrow driveway handling its curves with the ease of an expert driver. When her Chevy Blazer disappeared from view, Reese turned to Gretchen. "Well, girl, I guess that went well. What do you think?"

Gretchen wagged her tail and licked at Reese's outstretched hand.

CHAPTER 5

"Throughout the centuries we have projected on the wolf the qualities we most despise in ourselves."

- Barry H. Lopez, *Of Wolves and Men*

As days passed, Reese noticed the wolf's fur began to lose its sheen and become matted and knotted. It was obvious to him that its sagging hindquarters were ominous signs. The wolf's eyes, once brilliant green, began to haze over and the animal seemed to cling tentatively to life by drinking water, the only human offering it would take.

Whenever Gretchen was out of the cabin, she would go to the enclosure and bark at the stranger. When she neared the fence the wolf would approach her, stiffen and stand erect. It would not turn its head, but shifted its eyes to follow the dog's every movement. Then, slowly, as if trying to satisfy a curiosity, it would stretch its neck to nose the wire. With the wolf's first sniff, it appeared to Reese the animal recognized a familiarity because it would not counter aggressively.

Thereafter, whenever the wolf got the opportunity, it would limp closer to the dog, sniff at it through the fence and lay down nearby. Finally, Gretchen no longer barked at the wolf, but curled up close by and sniffed back. Reese took notice of the quick, mutual toleration between both animals.

This unexpected behavior of the two canids gave Reese an idea.

Just as he had since Gretchen was a pup, Reese spoke to the dog as though he were having a conversation with another person. "Gretchen, I know that wolf is not a man-eater; I'm not so sure about dogs. But when you go near the pen, he seems to like it. I think you can get him to eat. What do you think?"

Gretchen's tail flapped rapidly when she realized Reese was speaking to her. Waiting for a word or sign she recognized she became fully attentive, ears pitched forward and looking at Reese. To the dog, a command from her master was a chance to please, and she was not going to miss the opportunity.

Reese chuckled as Gretchen tilted her head and watched him closely. "If you understood what I had in mind, perhaps you wouldn't be so exuberant, young lady."

Reese grabbed a sack of fresh deer meat, leashed Gretchen and brought her to the enclosure, opened the gate and tethered her inside near the meat.

Gretchen fidgeted when Reese began to leave. "Now listen girl," he said calmly giving her shoulder a reassuring pat. "I know that wolf won't come over as long as I'm here, so I'm going to get out of sight. I'm not worried about you. With those stubby teeth and bad feet, he can't hurt you."

Reese stroked Gretchen's head. "Sit! Stay," he commanded. The obedient dog sat immediately and Reese glanced to the far corner of the enclosure. Like frosted glass orbs, lupine eyes were fixed on his every move.

Reese left the enclosure hoping his plan would work. He relied on the fact the wolf was not a more assertive alpha, but rather a less aggressive beta. What he counted on most was Gretchen's gender.

Trying more to convince himself, Reese talked to the dog as he backed away from the gate: "Now Gretch, just remember that male canids rarely hurt females despite the species."

Now that the dog was inside the pen with no human in sight, the wolf could inspect this creature with an odor more tolerable than any it had smelled since its captive ordeal began. It was a smell the wolf recognized from deep in its canid genes, and he crept toward the dog with its curiously familiar scent. Reese felt certain there was something in Gretchen's smell that made the wolf feel at ease. He was banking on the wolf's trust of the dog despite the lingering traces of scent from man's touch.

As the wolf drew near, Gretchen dropped to her front elbows and yipped softly. With her rump held high, she had the attitude of play in her body language and the signal of friendship in her wagging tail. The wolf recognized the look and slowly crept closer and closer, its tail tucked beneath it.

The wolf's neck fur was bottle-brushy, its ears pushed back and its nose extended toward Gretchen's. As their noses met, Gretchen came out of her crouch and the two distant cousins, stiffly and slowly, inspected each other. As in slow motion, the wolf's tail emerged from between its hind legs and stiffened out. Almost imperceptibly the tail moved. Then, slowly and methodically, it waved its canid hello.

For several moments the dog and the wolf tested scents both new and ancient, with Gretchen taking most of the initiative. The dog was playful with its lively step, the wolf more guarded with a stiffened stance, but between them, a peace was evident.

As Reese watched, Gretchen did what he hoped she would. She became interested in the meat, took a small chunk and gulped it down. Seeing this, the wolf crept toward the meat. It watched as Gretchen took a second chunk, but would not come closer. After the dog had eaten its fill, it hunkered down, licked its muzzle and stared at the wolf. The wolf became interested.

Lowering its body, the wolf inched forward and sniffed at the meat pile, straining to get closer without taking a step. Stretching its neck as far as it could the famished animal grabbed the nearest piece, then swiftly dragged it beyond the length of Gretchen's tether. There, the venison was swallowed without being chewed. Several times the wolf came back for hunks of meat, each time as cautiously as any omega would approach a feeding alpha. The dog tried to follow the wolf, but its leash held it back just as Reese had planned.

Finally, after weeks of severe hunger, the wolf had eaten.

Reese fed the wolf this way for several days. After a week, Reese found that he could be present as it came to eat. After a few more days the wolf seemed to become less frightened of Reese, and he could get closer to the enclosure whenever the two animals were together. Although the wolf seemed shy about doing so, it would come to the enclosure gate whenever Reese brought Gretchen in. As days went by, Reese would no longer tether Gretchen when he put her into the enclosure. Not only had Jeffrey Reese helped his dog attain the wolf's confidence, he was able to gain acceptance into the enclosure himself.

Still, the dog's behavior was beyond the wolf's comprehension. The animal liked Gretchen's company and tolerated Reese's presence, but it did not seem to understand why the dog chose to go to the human. The wolf realized the dog was free of its leash, but it still had trouble following the dog to the man. Every time Reese called Gretchen, the wolf would take a few steps to follow, but despite the dog's apparent joy to obey, the wolf kept its distance.

Trying to understand what Gretchen found appealing in the human scent, Dakota would sniff and lick the dog wherever Reese had touched, but Gretchen's fawning actions, although similar to his with his brother Bartok, seemed unacceptable to Dakota. It would take several more days with guarded trust before the wolf withstood the scent of the man. At least one more week would pass before Dakota would allow Reese within reach.

CHAPTER 6

"The wolf is one of nature's most fascinating creatures, ruthless hunter endowed with great intelligence and a striking ability to adapt."

- Anne Ménatory, ***The Art of Being a Wolf***

Elizabeth called a few times to see how Reese's doctoring was working. The phone conversations were usually long, both enjoying what the other had to say. She stopped by once and spent the afternoon watching him and Gretchen interacting with the wolf. When Reese came out of the enclosure, Elizabeth went over to him.

"Wow, what a great job you did. I can't believe how well he's doing," she said as she stood on her toes to reach up and peck a quick kiss on Reese's cheek.

He blushed. "What was that for?"

"A reward."

"I don't deserve it. Gretchen did most of the work."

When she saw his fluster, Elizabeth grinned. "I know, but she was farther away or I would have kissed *her*."

Reese laughed. He liked that Elizabeth made him feel as though he'd known her for years, and it was apparent that she was becoming fond of him. But he found it difficult to dismiss the sense of guilt that had him denying his feelings were mutual.

* * *

One evening while Reese was organizing his notes, the phone rang.

"Hello there, Jeff. Charley Whittington here. How are you doing?"

"Hey, Charley, I'm good. How's by you?"

"Good, good. Listen, one of the reasons I called was to see if you needed more meat, but more importantly, I spoke to Doc this afternoon and he says it's time to come over and remove the collar and casts from your wolf. We'll have to dart him, so I'll bring what I need."

There was a soft chuckle in Reese's voice. "Bring meat. It's all we'll need."

"What are you talking about?"

Reese paused, toying with the man. "You don't need to dart him."

"Why not?"

"Because they're off already."

"The collar fell off?"

"Everything's off. Collar, casts, everything."

"How'd that happen?"

Reese took a deep breath because he knew his answer was going to be shocking. "I took them off."

"You what?"

"I took the collar off a few days ago, and he unwrapped most of his own legs."

There was a long silence before Whittington said anything. When he did, it was spoken slowly, with an incredulous tone. "You removed the wrappings from the wolf's legs?"

"Uh huh. There wasn't a problem."

"Without darting him?"

"Yeah. I figured the darned thing suffered enough without traumatizing him any more."

Whittington's tone made it obvious that he wasn't convinced. "A wild wolf allowed you to touch it? I know his teeth are pretty well shot, but he can still rip you up with what he has left. How'd you do it?"

"You won't believe it, but Gretchen helped me make friends with him. I've been able to touch him for a week now. Especially after I took the collar off. When I did that, he seemed to trust me and then he let me take off what remained of the bandages."

"I don't believe it. I heard stories of people who've raised wolf cubs, but I never heard of anyone taming a wild one."

"Oh, no. No. I wouldn't say he's tame. And I don't think anyone else can touch him without Gretchen being there. She's probably the only reason I was able to get close enough."

"I guess that's good, but don't get too attached to that thing. You know we're going to have to release him soon."

"Trust me. I have no problem with returning him to where he belongs. I hate seeing him encaged like that."

"I do, too, Jeff. I like wolves, but I'd be careful if I were you. You never know what he might do. You just don't know."

"Not to worry. I'll be careful. --- Oh, before I hang up, do you know a John Dalton English?"

"J D? Yeah, I know him pretty good. John Dalton. Most folks in these parts know old J D English," said Whittington.

"What can you tell me about the guy?"

"Well, I suppose you should know that he's a huge wolf hater."

"I thought I heard something about that when I first came up here," said Reese. "So he's got pull, huh?"

"Heads up a group of ranchers who vow to do anything in their power to get rid of wolves. Including breaking the law if they have to."

"Great. Is that his claim to fame?"

"No. As a matter of fact, he's one of the wealthiest men in the state. Lives on one of the largest spreads around. Calls the place Elk Woods. Big drinker from what I understand. Why do you ask?"

"I met his daughter. She claims to disagree with him about de-listing wolves."

"If I were you, I'd stay clear of that one. People 'round here usually stick together. She might not like what old dad does, but she'd be hard pressed to take another side. He'd probably kill her if she did."

"That mean, huh?"

"Wasn't always. He kind of turned that way. Most people who knew J D years back knew a different man, well read, kind and generous to a fault. I guess he sees himself as less of a man since his wife made a cuckold out of him. Don't really know how Miss Beth puts up with him these days. His son left years ago. --- Yeah, if I were you I'd avoid ol' Dalton."

"Thanks for the advice," Reese said before ending the call.

* * *

The following weekend, Whittington, Doctor Ferris and two men from the Department of Conservation came to get the wolf and return it to the wild. When Reese accompanied the four men to the enclosure, the wolf bolted and rammed into the back end of the fence. The animal turned, cowered against the fence, and glared at the men with a crackling rumble deep in its throat that sounded more like a plaintive moan than a growl.

"How do you guys plan to do this," asked Reese.

"Well, unless you know a better way," Whittington said, "we're gonna have to dart him. How else can we get him in the crate?"

Turning to Ferris, Reese's question revealed his concern. "Doc, do we have to shoot a dart into him, or can we just give him a shot by hand?"

Looking into the enclosure, Ferris tilted his head down to peer over his reading glasses to make it obvious that he noticed the wolf was down on its belly as far away from the men as it could get. "Yes, we can, but by the looks of it, I don't think he's going to allow that. Do you?"

Reese saw Whittington shake his head, but he would not be discouraged. "Charley, I think I can give him the shot."

Whittington shrugged, raised his brow and looked at Ferris. The doctor glanced around at the other men before speaking to Reese. "That's up to you. Giving the injection is easy."

Whittington nodded his head. "I have no problem with it. Besides, I gotta see this."

Reese broke into a wide grin. "If you guys stay out of sight, Gretchen and I will take care of it."

After a brief lesson on administering a needle, Ferris, Whittington and the other men got out of sight. Reese called Gretchen and entered the pen. As soon as they were inside, Gretchen made a dash for the wolf, and it rose to meet her. Reese slowly approached as the dog and the wolf made their usual greeting: the dog, a sniffing Jell-O mold, shimmering with delight, the wolf, a gelid form, suspiciously sniffing back.

From several feet away Reese could see the wolf was not as calm as it usually became when it played with Gretchen. Shivering, it kept scanning the fence-line and glancing at Reese while trying to accept Gretchen's playful overtures. When Reese saw the wolf become more interested in Gretchen, he dropped to his knees and crawled slowly to get closer, extending his hand first toward the dog, then gently toward the wolf.

After nearly fifteen minutes, Reese could see the wolf was no longer trembling, and he was able to put a hand on its shoulder. Though Reese was shaking more than he anticipated, within a few more minutes he was able to calm his hand long enough to slip the needle into the wolf's fur. Reese was totally surprised that he didn't get bitten.

Allowing Gretchen to stay with the wolf, Reese carefully backed away. When he emerged from the enclosure the men waited for him to walk far enough from the pen before they came out of hiding.

Doc Ferris extended his hand. "Congratulations. I'm impressed. You should have been a veterinarian, Jeff. We could use one in the area."

Reese handed Ferris the syringe before shaking his hand. "That wasn't as easy as I thought it would be."

With his hands in his back pockets, Whittington stood wagging his head. "I can't believe what I just saw. I thought for sure you'd get bit."

"Want to know something Charley? So did I," said Reese looking into Whittington's eyes.

Ferris turned to Whittington. "I think wolves fear us above all other animals, don't you?"

"When it comes to man, there's something about the wolf I can't quite understand," Whittington said looking past the enclosure into the vast evergreen forest as if the distant wilderness held an answer. "The damned animal will fight a boar grizzly to the death to defend pups, yet an entire pack will run off if a single man raids its den."

"Not surprising," said Ferris.

Whittington shifted his gaze from Ferris to the tree line and again spoke to the forest. "Hell, I've talked with trappers who've approached a wolf in a leg trap. They tell of holding a hundred-pound male down with a stick, yet they say it takes two men with steel nerves and bludgeons to subdue a fifteen-pound bob cat."

Reese listened to the illogical truth. "I don't know. Maybe it's not fear as much as it is --- respect. Seems to me that wolves hold man to a different standard than they do the other animals."

"I wish I knew," said Whittington. "But I guess you're right. It seems to go beyond fear. It's as if they seem to know and consider our superiority."

"I do know this," Ferris said. "Except for the apes, compared to other animals wolves demonstrate more emotions and are far more intelligent. They're a lot like we are. I suppose that's why they've allowed us to domesticate them into dogs."

* * *

As soon as the shot took effect, Reese called Gretchen from the pen. Three men went in, lifted the tranquilized animal, muscled it into a crate and carried it to a pickup truck.

Whittington looked at Jeff Reese, but could not catch his eye. "Look, Jeff, we're going to stop and pick up the kid who trapped this guy so we can return him to where he was caught. Do you wanna come along?"

"No, Charley. You go on ahead. I'll hang out here and tend to Gretchen. She needs a little attention."

"Yeah. I'd say so. She sure did get upset when we put that wolf in the cage. Wow, I thought she'd have a fit."

"She'll be okay," Reese said looking toward the cabin where he had locked the dog while the men crated the wolf.

Ferris flopped a hand on Reese's shoulder. "I'm sure she'll be fine, but will you?"

When Reese smiled at Ferris, Whittington offered his hand to both men. "You two saved the animal's life."

"Jeff did everything," Ferris said.

Reese was silent for a moment as he gazed at the enclosure. "I enjoyed the whole experience. I'm sad to see him go, but glad he's on his way home."

“Me, too.” said Whittington. “Thanks again, Jeff.”

Reese watched the vehicles slowly rumble down the driveway until they were out of sight. He turned, took a long stare at the pen, and then went into the cabin to pet Gretchen.

Dakota was on his way back to Bass Creek, the very spot where he was caught.

CHAPTER 7

"For the strength of the pack is the wolf, and for the strength of the wolf is the pack."

- Rudyard Kipling, *The Jungle Book*

When Dakota awoke, his head ached and he fell as he tried to get up. After a few moments he stumbled dizzily to his feet, only to lose his balance and fall again. The wolf lay on its stomach for a while sniffing the air and glancing around.

Dakota felt thirsty and dizzy. But something else began to filter through cobwebs of confusion; something about his surroundings was eerily familiar. Slowly his head cleared and he began to realize his whereabouts.

Joy and fear overtook Dakota. The feeling of freedom rushed through him like a current, while a shock of fright bolted from his memory of this awful area. He staggered to his feet and wobbled awkwardly, but swiftly, away from the hellish place.

Before stopping at a small brook to drink, the wolf managed an unsteady gait until it was far enough away from where it had awakened. From the taste of the icy creek water sprang memories of dens, familiar wolves and brothers.

One of Dakota's first thoughts was of Bartok, and it righted his bearings. After a short rest, Dakota became more balanced and stronger as he trotted in a northerly direction, following instincts, following scents. He was following familiar trails. He was finally going home.

The lingering soreness in Dakota's legs prevented him from traveling as rapidly as he normally would have, but his progress was steady and direct. The determined wolf, nearly half way home, caught a fresh scent. Dakota stopped when he smelled it. He glanced around looking over his shoulder, and side to side. The scent, unmistakably, was that of a lone, male wolf, and Dakota bristled.

Old wars and territorial battles crossed his mind as he rechecked the odor of a strange wolf. Dakota knew the wolf that left the marker was not from his pack. He was certain he was in his old territory, Bartok's territory, but the marker suggested otherwise.

Dakota knew that no wolf would dare cross into Bartok's domain. If one did so by accident, it would not have left a marker. Scent signs were boundary indicators, and Dakota knew that his pack would fight another pack to the death to maintain them. The marker told him to keep out, and he was confused.

Still, he pushed forward. He had to find another marker, another sign that might indicate why a strange wolf had trespassed into what once was his domain. He ambled on, but slower, his pace tempered by a more cautious step.

It wasn't long before Dakota found what he had feared. As he slinked to the top of a rocky formation that formed a five-mile bench, he gained a vantage point from which he could survey a good portion of Bitterroot Valley, his former home. The lone wolf crawled to the brink of the great expanse, looked into the abyss of familiar surroundings and trusted his nose for the explanation.

The morning updrafts told Dakota everything he wanted to know, and the hair on his spine tingled to attention. A new pack of wolves had moved in, and as suddenly as he felt the exuberance of freedom, he felt the despair of disappointment. He was unfettered, yet he was bound tightly by the restrictions of his discovery. He was among wolves again, yet he was alone.

Dakota turned away. To be within the territory of a strange pack was certain trouble. Dakota knew he must get out before being detected. In no condition to defend himself, he obeyed his better judgment and plodded back toward the boundary he had crossed. When he reached the scent marker, he stopped, checked over his shoulder and urinated on the spot, a final defiance before crossing the boundary.

Dakota's ears drooped and his tail sagged. A dejected wolf, injured and alone, Dakota realized his perilous fate. He was aware that being infirm meant danger. He needed his pack. He missed his brother and wondered what had become of him. He could not understand why Bartok would have relinquished his domain.

For several days Dakota remained on the fringes of his old territory. He was beginning to feel the effects of hunger squeezing at his stomach. He hunted, but with his lack of speed, was unable to catch anything. Snowshoe rabbits were too fast, as were ground squirrels and cottontails. He searched the edges of ponds hoping to surprise the slower beavers, but he could not find a sign of a single one.

Four days passed before he was able to eat. He had stumbled upon a ptarmigan nest with a clutch of speckled eggs, and swallowed them whole. It was not a substantial meal, but it did sustain him until the next day when an afternoon breeze brought the smell of carrion across a bog to where Dakota caught the odor. His teeth were damaged and his legs unsound, but his nose was perfect. He followed the scent to the remains of a mountain lion kill and approached it only when his nose told him the cougar had not been there for a while.

Although the cat had eaten part of the deer, more than enough meat remained on the carcass to sate the wolf and nourish him for at least a week. Dakota stayed near the doe, eating and resting. The venison was a boon, but it did not come without a price. On the second day of Dakota's vigil over the kill, the cougar returned.

Dakota smelled the big cat before he saw it. It was a scent with which he was familiar, and he was aware that a mountain lion was more equipped to do battle using bone crushing fangs and flesh slitting claws. One swipe of the cat's paw could slash so deeply that it would kill, yet Dakota had minimal fear. The wolf's advantage over the cat was a superior brain. From past experiences Dakota knew that cats had far more fear of wolves and would avoid them even if it meant the loss of a life-sustaining meal.

The big cats were used to wolves being together, and every cat knew that a pack's fighting strategies were unbeatable for even the biggest cougar. No animal, regardless of its size, be it grizzly bear, bison or a bull elk with massive antlers, could challenge the strength of pack loyalty. It was devotion so intense that imminent death would not dissuade it, and mountain lions knew this well.

But Dakota was alone, and in his condition, he did not risk the challenge. He rose on his haunches and yipped several times before yowling to alert the cat. His warning served notice and the cougar, unaware the wolf was by itself, retreated swiftly.

Unfortunately, other more menacing ears heard Dakota's howl.

A hunting party of three wolves from the pack that made its home in Bartok's old territory was on the prowl. The wolves were not hunting for game; they were searching for a wolf. They had discovered the marker left by Dakota and were eager to punish the interloper.

The wolves were a half-mile away when they heard Dakota's yell. They broke into a trot and headed for their enemy. When the wolves got closer, they slowed to a zigzag approach, an effective tactic to locate their quarry by picking up its scent trail. When they did, they followed the spoor to the unsuspecting wolf. With the wind in their favor, the trio was able to get to within thirty yards of Dakota before he heard them.

Keen ears and the remains of the cougar kill spared Dakota's life. As hobbled as he was, when he heard the wolves, Dakota was able to bolt far enough away so the wolves became more interested in the remains of the deer than they were in him. The bounty was there for the taking and the wolves knew they could track Dakota again. A fight now was not to their advantage.

Dakota was aware the wolves did not want him near their territory. He knew they would resume their pursuit of him in due time. But he was alive and he would stay that way as best he could. He left the area for places unknown, but safer.

* * *

For the next two weeks Dakota ranged as far as he could from the dangerous pack. His travels took him miles away, but the more he roamed, the more he became further and further removed from the life he once knew and wanted back. Hunting voles and field mice to keep alive, he was becoming desperate to be with a pack.

Dakota wanted the company of wolves; he wanted to hunt with

them, play with them and be comforted by them. He missed the affection of his kind and he craved their touch. He wanted to live with them again. Although he searched for his own pack, he just wanted to be with wolves. He made a decision to return to where he last knew them to be.

Although his legs were getting stronger, they were not completely sound and it took several days to get back to where he last knew of wolves. It was the middle of June by the time he returned and picked up the scent of wolves. Dakota's muscles tightened. His silver mane stood up. The skin on his neck tingled, sending waves of rippling fur over his shoulders and along his spine. Dakota realized the scent he found was that of the wolves that had chased him.

Resigned to gamble his life in order to be accepted, Dakota crossed the boundary into his old territory. As he approached, the scent of wolves was fresh, but the surroundings he entered were more foreboding than any wolves he might encounter. Still, he pressed on, slowly recognizing pieces of habitat, bits of terrain, a chewed lodgepole pine stump and an aura of tragedy. He was back, back to where the nightmare of his present life had begun. He had returned to the terrible place. The place where he last saw his brother.

Though horror surrounded him, so did the memory of Bartok, and Dakota decided to stay. He knew that if ever he were to find Bartok again, if ever he were to find life again, it would be in this place.

Raising his head to the heavens, Dakota howled. The woeful baying boomed through the balsams and tamaracks, rumbled over ridges and crags, rolled down the rivers and streams to settle into the soul of the Bitterroots.

It was only a matter of time before three wolves came across Dakota's scent. They recognized the smell and at once took pursuit. When they heard his howl they quickened their pace to find Dakota. They would kill him when they did. Dakota would face them and try to befriend them if he could.

It took twenty minutes before the wolves were facing Dakota. As soon as he saw the marauders, Dakota lowered his head and slivered to his belly trying to appeal to their mercy. The malevolent three growled viciously, baring their teeth and snarling. Saliva glistened on their fangs. The wolves were serious about their intent, nasty and deliberate. An alien wolf was in their territory and had to be removed for the good of their own pack.

Dakota crooked his tail between his hind legs and avoided eye contact with the strangers, but despite his submissive gestures, these wolves were not willing to accept him. Dakota knew it immediately, but it was too late. He had allowed killers to get too close. Dakota was surrounded and he bawled again, long and loud, ringing soulfully to distant hills.

CHAPTER 8

"To isolate a wolf from its pack is tantamount to torture."
- Jim Dutcher, *Wolves at Our Door*

Idaho summer came late to the Bitterroots. Shako's pups, anxious to get out of the den, played tag in the warmth of the June sunshine as Bartok and Anoki, an old, pure white female looked on. The rest of the pack had drifted off to a nearby glade in order to avoid the incessant pestering of the youngsters. It was early in the day when the first bawl rang out.

Even at a great distance, the pack had little difficulty hearing the call. Bartok sprang to his feet and snarled at the yipping pups to quiet them. He cocked his head to listen for what he thought was a distress call. Shako, too, heard the yell, but being distracted by the pups, she did not identify the uniqueness of its tone.

It was impossible for the pups to restrain themselves for any length of time. Restless to resume their play, they began to yip again, romping with each other, tumbling and squealing loudly. Again, Bartok scolded, snarling at the pups until Shako and Anoki escorted the pups away from their father. Shako sensed uneasiness in her mate and she and Anoki left his side with the pups trailing and nipping at their tails. Bartok listened again.

The big male became restive, pacing back and forth. There was something about the howl he had heard that spurred his decision to leave. Bartok trotted away in the direction of his old den site.

The black wolf quickened his pace. The closer Bartok got to his previous territory, the more rapidly he scampered. When he reached his destination at the edge of his former boundary, he stopped. Unfamiliar odors filled the air. He bristled at the smell of wolf urine marking the territory, a sign that a new pack had taken residency in his old home.

Respecting the markers, Bartok backed away. He did not want a confrontation with wolves defending their territory. When he got to a safe distance from the boundary, he sat back on his haunches to rest. That's when he heard it again, a long bellow, soulful and clear. It was a howl that he had not heard in months, but it had a familiar urgency with a pitch of fear. The sound came from the direction of Dakota's tragic event and Bartok bolted into a sprint.

* * *

Dakota was surrounded. Three wolves growled violence at the intruder as he cowered against the huge, lodgepole stump. With enraged wolves threatening him, Dakota bellowed. Fear raised the hackles on the nape of his neck. There was no way he could defend himself. With only one chipped fang and two fragile legs, he knew that a single wolf could defeat him easily; three would mean instant disaster.

Dakota wanted to run, but with an infirm gait he knew he could not outrun the wolves. He was trapped. Trapped in the very place where he had been trapped before. He looked at the malicious wolves and did not have to wonder what kind of enemy these jawed monsters were that cornered him. As he had looked at a deadly spring trap that nearly took his life, he looked at these enemies as growling and snarling death. Dakota would engage in another war all the more perilous.

The three infuriated wolves inched closer when Dakota glanced desperately beyond them. He saw something. Powdery dirt billowed on the horizon. Something was streaking from behind the three menacing wolves on a direct line toward Dakota. In a cloud of breath and rolling dust came a charging, black speck, growing larger and larger as it closed. Closer, the speck grew into a form, and closer, the form grew into a wolf. At break-neck speed the wolf was only yards away when Dakota recognized him.

Bartok!

At full blast, Bartok slammed into the largest of the three antagonists, sending it sprawling and running for its life. Turning to the other wolves, Bartok focused his anger and charged.

Yelping and growling ferocity, fang, fur and fury collided as Dakota flung into the fray, snarling and snapping into a whirling mass of stabbing teeth, slashing, biting, ripping and tearing. Bartok would not need his brother's help in the fight, but Dakota's loyalty, as devoted as the bond of conjoined twins, would make short work of the melee and ensure victory. Within seconds, the war was over. The beaten wolves scattered and ran, yelping their defeat.

Dakota felt the last of his strength dissipate as an instant limpness took over his body. The fight had drained the last of his energy, and he felt weakness even more severe than when he was encaged. Months of the worst ordeal of his life were over, but the price had exacted its toll.

Before the defeated wolves reached the horizon, quietude replaced the sounds of the fight in Dakota's ears. It was as if the din of a thunderous battle had deafened him and he wilted in the eerie silence, muted even to the sound of his own breathing. Shakily he watched as Bartok took several bounds in pursuit of the fleeing wolves before stopping. Certain that his enemies were gone, Bartok turned to his brother.

When the two wolves made eye contact, Dakota's vitality began to return. He had always felt his brother's devotion, and now, more than ever before, he drew from the power of Bartok's presence. Like a surge of adrenaline, Dakota could feel strength well from his chest, rush through his veins and flood into his muscles. He knew that he would never again have to endure another hardship as long as he had Bartok in his life.

With canid body language the brothers converged. Bartok nuzzled Dakota, inspecting for wounds and found only a scratch. Dakota soothed cuts on Bartok's shoulder. Confident that neither was badly hurt, the brothers licked sloppily at each other, squealing and yipping like puppies, rolling over and sidling up to each other, reveling in their ecstasy. Both wolves were so vigorous in showing their jubilance they exhausted themselves demonstrating it.

After a short rest, the two wolves again shared affectionate gestures, licking and sniffing. Dakota, rolling to his back, turned his underbelly to his alpha brother in a display of subservience. Bartok, massive jaws agape, poked playfully at Dakota's snout as he stood over him in a show of dominance. Finally the wolves stood nose to nose until they both stopped panting. Then Bartok turned from his brother, looked homeward and trotted off in that direction with Dakota following. Without looking back, Bartok led the way. It was Dakota who paused as he crested a knoll and stopped. He took a final look behind at a place he would never forget, nor to which he would ever return. Then, the magnificent gray wolf swung into a run to catch up with the ebony savior.

Despite the sophistication of his body language and the multiple meanings of his vocalizations, Dakota could not tell the wolves of his pack where he had been or how he was able to return. He could never tell Bartok and the pack that man was responsible. Although the wolves of the pack had keen memories of Dakota, they held no curiosity about his absence. What mattered to Bartok and his wolves was that Dakota was back. Though Dakota had broken teeth, his legs would become sound again, and all that mattered to him, too, was that he was back.

Once again, the wolves were reunited and that was all that mattered to any of them.

CHAPTER 9

"We do not like ambiguity; we like black or white, not gray. Wolves come in many shades of gray. We need only to follow them, for it is we, not they, who have forgotten how to navigate the 'gray areas'."

- Renee Askins, *Shadow Mountain*

With his dog lying on the front seat next to him, Jeffrey Reese drove through a morning mist. He wanted to get to Doc Ferris as fast as he could, but the heavy fog would not oblige; it hung in the still air like a damp, gauze curtain. Reese choked the steering wheel and cursed the foul weather. Gretchen had been acting strangely for several days, and when she stopped eating, Reese became worried. He tried nursing the dog during the night, staying awake to comfort its apparent distress.

The dog whimpered as Reese probed its abdomen. "Hold on girl. We'll be there in a minute."

Squinting into the cloud, Reese gripped the wheel tightly with his left hand as he stroked his dog's stomach with the other. "What the heck did you get into Gretch? Some kind of bad meat or something?"

Gretchen turned her head painfully to lick her master's hand as if she realized he was fretting for her.

As Reese pulled into Ferris's driveway, the doctor was already out of the door to meet him. "Jeff, why didn't you call me earlier?"

"I didn't want to wake you during the night, Doc. Bad enough I got you out of bed."

A good-humored man with a trustworthy disposition, Doctor Andrew Ferris was one of the people who lived near Stevensville whom everyone depended upon. "No sweat," Ferris said. "Had to get up anyway."

"I know it's before visiting hours," Reese said as he helped Ferris lift Gretchen and carry her into the office.

"Just as well. I'm not so sure my regular patients would like to see me tending to a dog."

"Sorry, but isn't it about time they got a vet in the area?"

"Hey, I'm only kidding," Ferris chided. "Folks in these parts wouldn't mind a bit. Now the medical association is a different kettle of fish, but if you don't tell 'em, I won't."

Reese forced a faint smile. "Thanks Doc. My lips are sealed."

Ferris began to examine Gretchen and Reese described his dog's symptoms. "I think she may have eaten some poison or something. She seems to be in pain and she's really sensitive when I touch her gut. But, you know, I don't know how that could happen. She never wanders far from the property."

Examining the dog, Ferris held up his hand to quiet Reese. After a pause, the doctor removed the stethoscope from his ears and stared solemnly at Reese. "I guess you're worried stiff, right?"

"Yeah, I'm worried. She seems pretty bad," Reese said as he tried to read the doctor's expression. "Is she going to be okay?"

"Did you think you were going to lose your dog?"

Shaking his head slowly, Reese studied Ferris's face but didn't answer. Doc Ferris was one of the first people Reese met in Montana, yet, since first seeing the man, Reese noticed a peculiarity that he attributed to bedside manner. The doctor's cherubic cheeks coaxed the bottom of his eyelids into a slant, and his slightly arched brow and bowed up lips framed a jolly face. Looking to Ferris for a telling facial expression was futile; the man seemed to have a permanent smile that prevented any preconception of his examination.

But Reese's heart lightened when Ferris broke into a laugh. "You know, for an educated man, you're pretty naive. You're not going to lose a dog. You're going to gain a few. Miss Gretchen, here, is in labor. She's going to have puppies!"

"She's pregnant?"

"Yes, she is."

"How the heck did that happen?"

"I already said you were naive," Doc giggled. "Please tell me I don't have to answer that."

"I know *how*. I meant how could it have happened?"

"You let her in with that male wolf you had a couple of months ago, right?"

"You don't think that ----?"

"Well, you wanted her to make friends, didn't you?"

Again, Jeffrey Reese looked at Doc Ferris in disbelief. "I didn't think that was possible."

"What? That she'd make friends?"

"No. That she'd mate with a wolf."

"She's a canine, isn't she? Well, so is he, and they can breed with each other. You should know that."

"I do know it's possible. I just didn't know she was going to get that friendly." Reese couldn't contain a smile. "I watched them most of the time and I never saw anything to suggest it could happen."

"Unless there was another dog around, it happened," Doc's perpetually bowed up lips morphed into a wholesome grin. "I think canines gestate for about nine weeks. You do the math."

"No, Doc. No dogs were ever around."

Reese changed the subject. "How come she wasn't showing? She didn't look pregnant."

Ferris tilted his head, "I don't think she's carrying more than two or three pups. I don't know for sure, but usually young dogs like Madam Gretchen, here, don't have large litters the first time, so it's possible to not notice. But an x-ray will show all that."

Ten minutes later, the doctor slid an x-ray onto the lighted wall box and pointed out three perfectly formed pups.

"I'm no obstetrician, but my diagnosis was pretty accurate. They look a little on the small side to be of term. That's probably why you couldn't tell."

Reese combed his fingers through his hair and laughed. "Now what do I do?"

"Well, what do you want to do? It's too late to terminate the pregnancy, but you can get rid of them after."

Reese's sky-blue eyes became serious. "I wouldn't do that. I couldn't do that!"

"Well, to be honest, from what I know, wolves don't make very trustworthy pets."

"They're only half wolf," Reese protested, "Gretchen's demeanor is in there, too. Besides, that wolf was not that aggressive. I was able to touch the darned thing. Remember?"

"Well, it's up to you. Gretchen's your dog and you can do what you want. Personally, I wouldn't want to make that decision, either. I'd probably keep the dang things, too, especially if I were up in the woods where you live."

"I'm not going to be there forever, but this whole thing is kind of my fault, so I guess I'll have to keep the pups."

"If I were a gambler, that would have been my bet."

Doc stroked Gretchen's head. "I know how much you love having this dog around, so why not increase the company?"

As Reese bent down to kiss the side of Gretchen's muzzle, Doc offered some parting advice. "You'll be in for some work for the next couple of hours, but after the first one, the next two shouldn't be more than a half hour apart."

Thankful the fog had lifted, both from the roadside and his mind, Reese drove Gretchen back to his cabin and made her as comfortable as possible. As hour after hour passed, Reese sensed something was wrong. After a grueling twelve-hour vigil, Gretchen delivered her first puppy. The newborn was not breathing as Reese took it into his hands to clear its mouth. He dried the tiny pup with a towel and rubbed it gently trying to get it to take a breath, but the jet-black male did not survive long enough to be with its sister born a half-hour later.

Jeffrey Reese struggled to tend to the new arrival while Gretchen labored to deliver the last puppy. Reese had the female pup cleaned, dried and searching for its first meal at the tip of his little finger when Gretchen began to moan and whimper painfully.

Wrapping the puppy in a dry towel, Reese placed it into a cardboard box and then attended to the whining Gretchen. "Hang in there, girl. One more and it's all done."

Reese glanced at the wall clock. It was nearly 3:AM. He realized that more than two hours had passed since the last pup was delivered.

Kneeling close to his dog, Reese put a water-soaked cloth to Gretchen's muzzle and squeezed the cool liquid into her mouth. She swallowed with difficulty and then tried to get to her feet. Reese held her down, but thought he had made a mistake as the dog vomited the water and began to convulse repeatedly. Reese's concern grew more intense, sweat soaked his shirt collar and his heart was a jackhammer blasting at his chest.

Gretchen no longer whimpered though her pain was obvious. Reese's worry turned into fear. His dog meant everything to him and he could not imagine what his life would be without her companionship.

"Miss Gretchen, you're scaring me to death. C'mon, girl. Get that pup out, please."

Reese looked at the clock again and groaned when he discovered that another hour had passed. "God. It's been hours now. What the heck's happening here?"

Turning his attention from Gretchen, Reese checked on the restless puppy. It squirmed and mewed barely audible cries as Reese comforted it.

"You must be hungry little girl, but your mother is a bit busy right now. You'll have to wait a while."

Reese took the pup from its wrap and brought it close to its mother's muzzle. Gretchen tried feebly to lick her puppy, but her dry tongue would not allow her the pleasure. When Reese saw how dehydrated Gretchen was, he panicked. He put the puppy next to its mother, got more water and struggled again to get his dog to drink.

Reese could feel that Gretchen was burning up. "You've got fever. What can I do for you? Ice! I'll make an ice pack for you, Gretch. Just hold on girl; please hold on."

Jeffrey Reese was reliving a nightmare, a morbid dream. A young wife, in complicated labor with her first child, dies with her baby so many years ago. Three lives destroyed in an instant, two mercifully gone, the third left to suffer the torment of unrelenting memory and long nights of fitful sleep.

When Reese returned with the ice pack, he found the puppy had wriggled to its mother's warmth and in its blindness found where to suckle. Gretchen looked up at Reese, made a double thump with her tail and in an exhaustive effort, nestled her head in his extended hand

and breathed a sigh. Reese held his dog's head on his lap, spoke softly to her, and stroked her gently as she gasped for air. He feared with every labored breath the dog took.

Within an hour, Gretchen was dead.

CHAPTER 10

"Wolves are not our brothers; they are not our subordinates, either. They are another nation, caught up just like us in the complex web of time and life."

- Henry Beston, Naturalist

Reese wanted to choose an appropriate gravesite, but could not do it. None seemed right to him. No place deserved his beloved dog. No place in the ground. Again, guilt was a dank cloak enveloping him and he could not shed it. Were it not for him, Gretchen would be alive. Wretchedness erupted from the pit of his stomach and spewed upward into his chest, swirling and churning. Then, a blunted vacuum tube punched through his ribcage to suck out the contents of his soul. Reese was left with a void as vacant as a lifeless abyss, a cavity that would refill only with the torments of past misery.

Shrouded in morning mist, his mind clogged with bad memories, Reese dug the grave on a hillside above the cabin. Again he had lost a loved one and the pain was sickeningly reminiscent. He thought of Samantha and how much he missed her. Now, he would have to be without Gretchen. The mere thought of it stabbed into his breast like a frozen sword and his heart bled. He felt the fluid of life push upward, choke into his throat and flow into his head where it seeped from his eyes to trickle down his cheeks.

As he began to lay the pregnant dog into the cool earth, Reese thought that at last now his dog's fever would abate. He gently placed the stillborn pup under Gretchen's chin, removed his coat and wrapped them both with his favorite parka. Jeff Reese was not burying Gretchen and her pup; he was burying his heart.

The painful task finished, Reese said a prayer. "I never understood you Lord, and I'm not sure I ever will. If there's no place for dogs in heaven, I'd ask not to be invited, but then I'd miss seeing Sammy again.

I don't know where it is that Gretchen and her pups will go, but I'd wish that I could visit there at least one time. Please look over her soul, Lord; it was one of the sweetest You ever made."

Despite having been awake for two days, sleep was impossible. He needed someone to talk with. For a moment he wished he had Elizabeth's number, but a stirring sensation crept from his stomach, pulsed through his chest and pushed up into his head forcing the thought from his mind, and he allowed that he couldn't contact her. Jeffrey Reese had not been in Montana long enough to make close friends, but Doc Ferris was one of the men he liked and trusted as a confidant. Cradling the surviving puppy on his lap, he picked up the phone and dialed the doctor's number.

"Hello Doc, it's Jeff."

"Hello, Jeff. How's it going?"

Reese choked out the words to tell Ferris about Gretchen, and the doctor could feel the man's heartache through the telephone. Doc knew what Gretchen meant to Reese, and he also knew about the tragedy of his friend's past. Words would be of little comfort, so Ferris used only a few to express his sorrow and then spoke of a different topic. "Tell me about the pup that made it."

Shrugging a shoulder, Reese trapped the phone to his ear to free his hands and lifted the tiny animal close enough to his face to smell the sweetness of its breath. "She's the reason I called. Seems healthy, but I'm not sure I know what to do with her."

"Listen, Jeff, I have no patients scheduled for the rest of the day," Ferris lied. "Why don't you bring that puppy down so I can have a look at it? We'll figure out something, okay?"

After he got Reese to agree to bring the puppy to him, Doc finished treating the patients who were in his office and asked his wife to call and cancel the remaining visits for the day.

When Reese arrived, Doc made a fuss over the puppy and

examined it. "I'm not too well versed in veterinary science, but it seems like she's strong enough, Jeff. Right now she's got antibodies in her system from Gretchen, but in a few weeks she'll need some shots. I'll do some research to get what I need for her by then, but here are some things you need to pick up."

As he handed a small list to Reese, Ferris asked if his wife could see the puppy. The doctor knew what to say to lift Reese's spirits. "Martha is a sucker for puppies. She'd never forgive me if I didn't allow her to see this little girl after all my fussing. But under no circumstances do you allow her to talk you into giving her the pup. Deal?"

Reese glanced at the pup. His face, haggard by fatigue, untwisted into its usual pleasant countenance. "It's a deal," he said.

When Reese left Doc Ferris's office, he drove into town to buy the suggested items. He picked up a few things along with a baby bottle, evaporated milk, several pints of heavy cream, and then headed for his cabin feeling burdened about what he had to do. He was ambivalent about having another pet. He wanted Gretchen, not a wolf-dog. But he felt that he owed at least as much to Gretchen to raise her only offspring.

Reese neglected his magazine work. He had to get out into the field and report on the wolves that were released around the Idaho/Montana border. Not familiar with the area, he needed to find an experienced guide to help him locate wolves. Now that he had first-hand experience that unmarked wolves lived in the nearby mountains, he had to get back to the project, but he felt obligated to stay with Gretchen's puppy.

After his wife's death, he fought to free himself of the wretched feeling of total loneliness. When alcohol, his narcotic substitute, failed, he surrounded himself with family and friends. But even among those he loved, the darkness grew. It took nearly a year for the festering wound that despondency opened to finally heal, but it was not without scars.

Now it had returned. Back was that sickness, that lonesomeness, as though he were being drawn into a downward spiral of bleakness once again with no one to pull him up. And now, the scars began to show. Those ghostlike memories that distorted his perceptions made Reese guard against the return of the awful gloom, the dreaded loneliness.

Reese was in a state of despair, like being alone when he most needed companionship, like falling into the darkness of a bottomless pit when he most needed light. He was in a mindset similar to that which he felt upon the loss of Samantha, when Elizabeth English phoned.

Reese rejected any attempt at tenderness from a woman. Samantha's death was Jeffrey Reese's ultimate tragedy. No pain could be more intense, no miseries more despairing. When that grief stabbed into his life, it was *his* red badge to display. For Reese, an acceptance of comfort was recognition that a healing process was possible, and signified that he was willing to let go of that which he had dearly needed most in his world.

With Elizabeth's call, the scars from his past were colloid reminders, making Reese's reaction distort into a wall of protection. He told her about Gretchen and the puppy, yet was angry when she suggested she visit.

He squeezed the receiver wanting to grab the woman and drag her into his despondency. Reese raised his voice to a level that even stunned him. "I don't think it's a good idea for you to come here now. I don't need help. I don't want company right now, and I sure as hell don't care to hear about another anti-wolf demonstration that your father is planning."

Elizabeth groped for words. "I. I'm so sorry, Jeff. Please forgive me."

There was line-dead silence from the phone, unearthly and still, as though Reese had been sucked into oblivion by a giant vacuum tube. He knew he had hurt her, but he had no way to explain feelings he himself could not understand.

Shaken by Reese's ill-spirited coolness and the dreadful news about Gretchen, Elizabeth became overly cautious with her words. "You have no idea how sorry I feel. I wish I could help somehow."

After another mute pause, Elizabeth realized there was nothing more to say and she attempted a dignified ending to the call: "I have a new cell phone. I guess it's not a good time to take my number, so I'll mail it to you in case you'd like to speak with me again. I am truly sorry, Jeff."

Reese mustered a weak response. "Yeah, Beth. Me, too."

Elizabeth said goodbye, but Reese couldn't bring himself to say it back. When she hung up, Reese heard the conclusive click of the receiver and the finality of quietude clogged his ears. He kept holding the phone to his ear as though hoping her voice would somehow re-emerge, and he hung up only when the blaring alarm of the off-the-hook-signal jolted him into the realization of what he had just done.

Filled with uncertainty, his head began to throb. Reese kneaded his temples as conflicting thoughts jabbed into his brain and began to spar. Good and bad thoughts first pushed at each other, then shoved until they seemed to engage in an all-out brawl. It seemed to Reese as if a dogfight began in his skull. Not like a World War II air battle between Zeroes and Flying Tigers, but an all-out fracas between vicious junkyard mongrels, snarling and snapping at one another.

Bad thoughts fought in, scratching and clawing with a vigor fueled by Gretchen's death. These thoughts fought a sordid fight, their slings, energized by the guilt Reese felt for allowing the wolf to be with Gretchen. Bad thoughts about Samantha's death, and more guilt added to his confusion.

Some good thoughts came swirling in, twisting and gliding into the fray. The puppy was a part of Gretchen and he took comfort in that. Elizabeth English was one of the more pleasant beings he had gotten to know and he was beginning to like her. Yet when he tried to reason why he had spoken to her as he had, he felt trapped by uncertainty and sought to escape the bewilderment, like a butterfly escapes its cocoon.

Reese looked to his work for refuge, and as days passed he wrote a few articles about the wolf he had nursed and released back into the wild. He also sent in an illuminating piece about the misconceptions most people have about wolves, but most of his time was spent raising the pup, and the remainder of it mourning Gretchen.

CHAPTER 11

"To look deeply into a wolf's piercing eyes is a stirring experience that demands honesty."

- Helen Thayer, *Three Among Wolves*

A week went by and Reese received a letter from Elizabeth. A faint, quick thumping in his chest suggested more than he was willing to admit as he opened the short note. Along with another apology, she had written her phone number and a few words telling him he could call whenever he chose. He looked at the number and resisted the urge to pick up the phone.

The scars of past memories had not disappeared.

It was around this time the dreams began. At first they were only shaded images, vague visions of Samantha and Gretchen. He would see them both at a distance. The visions were always the same; Samantha and the dog would be coming to him, but they'd never reach him.

As time passed, the dreams began to recur and become more elaborate, painful and cruel. He'd hear Samantha calling to him from the dark. He could hear Gretchen's whimpers of need. He could not see them; he could hear Sammy's voice and Gretchen's bark, but he could not call back. Samantha would scream his name, begging him to answer. He tried to respond, but his voice stuck in his throat and would not come out. Mumbling, he'd try shouting, only to awaken himself with hideous squeals to find Gretchen's puppy at his bedside yipping at him. He loathed those dreams. He feared them and hated to fall asleep. These grotesque, recurring nightmares were as frightening to Reese as the thought of his own demise.

Several more weeks passed before Reese had a visitor. He had refused all company, but late one afternoon a boy on horseback rode to the edge of Reese's property, tied his mount to a sapling and shuffled to the door. Reese was curious when he saw the boy. He knew most of the people in and around Stevensville, but he did not recognize the bronze-skinned youth.

With a tentative step and darting glances the boy made an uneasy approach to the door, but did not knock. He could hear the puppy yipping, and realized it was announcement enough. He stood stiffly; his only movement was the fumbling of a tattered cowboy hat in his hands until Reese came to the door.

When Reese opened the door, the boy stepped back and Reese got a better look at the young Indian. The sixteen-year-old's blue-black hair shined as if it were shellacked. The sheen of double braids framing his face reflected onto the smooth copper skin of prominent cheekbones, an unmistakable feature of his race. Above the cheekbones, serious dark eyes were penetrating, intelligent, yet fearful.

Reese stepped out onto the porch. "How can I help you young man?"

Reese's voice sounded strange to himself. Except for a few words to the pup, it had been over eight weeks since he had spoken at all.

"Are you Mister Jeffrey?" the boy asked meekly while torturing the hat.

"I'm Jeff Reese."

"My name's Jacy Cayuse. Friends call me Jay."

Reese sensed the boy's nervousness. "Crowe? Blackfoot?" he asked.

"No sir," came a quick reply.

Reese saw the boy's face brighten. Though there was little hint of mirth, his expression exuded pride. "Nez Perce," he said as he looked straight at Reese for the first time.

"Well, Jay, what can I do for you?"

Jacy's eyes again turned toward his fistful of crumpled western hat. “I’m. I. I caught the lobo. The wolf you had here in springtime.”

“So you’re the one who caused all this?”

As soon as he uttered the words, Reese saw the boy flinch, look down at the hat he held and squeeze it. Realizing the message the boy heard was not the meaning he intended, Reese wanted to say he was kidding. Facetiousness, though, was too difficult to explain, so Reese merely changed his tone. “I’m glad you came. As a matter of fact, I’ve been meaning to look you up for the longest time.”

The boy wrinkled his nose. “Me?”

“Uh, huh. I think you may have some information that could help me with my work. Where’re you from?”

“I live on tribal lands. I know ‘bout your trouble and I come to see you and the wolf cub. Is it okay?”

Reese invited the boy in. “How did you hear about the pup? It’s not all wolf, you understand.”

“Yessir. I know. I hear from Mister Joe. Mister Joe Morton.”

The boy searched the room, glancing in the corners, his eyes squinting to adjust to the low light. “Where’s the puppy?”

“She’s in the back room. Likes to run outside, so I put her away when I heard you come to the door.”

Reese turned to let the pup out. “Brace yourself. She gets excited.”

The pup nearly tripped over itself trying to get to the boy. Flipping his hat to the floor, Jacy dropped on his knees to pet the yipping ball of fur. It immediately rolled onto its back and squealed delight as the youngster rubbed its underbelly.

“I kin tell it ain’t no alpha. What’s its name?”

Reese didn’t have an answer. For nearly two months he had nurtured the animal from a runt-scrawny specimen to a healthy pup, but never named it. It was an intentional overlook. He didn’t want to get too attached. Naming the pup seemed to him an acceptance of Gretchen’s replacement, and he couldn’t do it.

Reese was embarrassed that he had no name. “I was still searching for a good one. Maybe you can help me with it.”

“I know ‘bout your dog dying.” Jacy’s voice trailed off as his eyes fixed on the puppy. “What was her name?”

“Gretchen.” Reese paused reverently. “She was my rock, my angel, but I can’t use that name.”

The boy flashed a generous smile that uncovered gleaming teeth, white and perfectly shaped, save a slight space between the top front two. "But you have a name," he said. "You said it."

"What do you mean?"

"Nitika! Nitika means angel of precious stone. It's from Nez Perce. Nitika is the best name you kin find. Angel of precious stone," Jacy repeated.

"Well, then, Nitika it is," Reese announced. "I like it. Thank you, Mister Jay."

Jacy beamed. "You're welcome." More warmth than pride radiated from his face. No one had ever addressed him as Mister, at least no white man. The boy had made an instant friend, and he began to feel more at ease as he sprawled on the floor toying with the newly named pup.

Reese eyed Jacy with curiosity. "Tell me something. You said that Nitika, here, wasn't an alpha. How do you know that?" Reese already knew the answer, but he wanted to know how much Jacy knew about wolves.

"Alphas don't turn their bellies up. Only a beta or omega does. Not even a she-wolf or girl dog does."

Reese was impressed. "You know something, Jay? You could really help me. How well do you know the forest area where you trapped that wolf?"

"I know it real good. Bass Creek ain't far from where I bin trappin'. Bin trappin 'roun' there a long time."

"Did you know there was a wolf pack up there?"

Jacy pried his attention away from Nitika, picked up his hat, rose slowly to his feet and examined the floor. "I knew 'bout the pack," he confessed. "I was after a wolverine that was stealin' from my trap line. I caught that lobo. I didn't think I would catch no wolf, but when I seen him in the trap, I knew I done bad. Shouldn't a set a big trap. I like wolves. I know 'bout 'em. I wish I had a wolf. I'm sorry for what I done."

Reese could feel the boy's remorse. It resembled a darkness with which he was familiar. "I like them, too, but unfortunately a lot of folks have different impressions about the animal. That's part of the reason I'm here."

"Joe tol' me what you was doin' here. I didn't mean to hurt that wolf. I hope nobody ever hurts one of 'em again. They was forced out of these hills just like…"

The boy bit into his lip and stared at Reese expecting to get scolded.

Jeff Reese finished the boy's thought: "Just like your ancestors were. You don't have to be afraid to say it, son. It's a fact. People mistreated Native Americans and there's not much anyone can do to change that, but maybe we can change it for the wolves."

Jacy couldn't make eye contact. He kept looking down at the pup tugging at his pant leg. "I'm glad that lobo is okay now," he said slowly lifting his eyes to meet Reese's.

Reese felt the discomfort. "Where did all this good feeling about wolves come from, Jay?"

Jacy's eyes widened and he began to speak more rapidly. "From my people. Nez Perce people was always with wolves. When wolves was let go in Yellowstone, one bunch was called Chief Joseph pack. Chief Joseph was a Nez Perce chief."

Reese wondered at the boy's enthusiasm. "That was in '96," he said. "I think the Chief Joseph pack was four wolves of the seventeen released that year."

Jacy nodded. "Yes, and a bigger bunch was called Nez Perce pack. Nez Perce word for wolf is *shon tonga.* Taborri, mother of my father, tol' me stories 'bout *shon tonga.*"

Reese listened as Jacy related a story of his ancestors and their fondness for wolves. Where truth and fantasy divided seemed obvious to Reese, but to Jacy the tale carried a legend he appeared to hold sacred.

"Taborri tol' me," Jacy said. "A half-breed baby was left by her people to die in the mountains. A wolf pack found the baby. The wolves took it to their den. One day a Indian brave was huntin' and he found it and brang it back to his camp.

Taborri said the people did not want the baby. They made the brave go live in the mountains. He took the baby and his family to live with the wolves."

As Reese listened, he gathered that Indian tribes and generations, too numerous to count, passed the legend down to the children of the Nez Perce.

"Mister Jeff, Taborri picked my name because it was the name of her father. He was hanged when he let free a *shon tonga* that was caught in a white man's snare. I can never hurt a wolf. I feel bad 'bout what I done."

"Well, how would you like to make up for what you did?"

The boy stared at Reese, and then glanced down at Nitika. "I'll do anything."

"I'd like you to take me up to that area where you caught the wolf. I'd like to look around. Do you think you can guide me?"

"Most sure I can, Mister Jeff. Honest!"

After making arrangements to meet Jacy, Reese watched the boy dash to his mustang, vault over its rump onto its bare back and gallop off with a screechy, "aaaayeeee!" He whooped until he was out of sight.

Reese bent down to pick up the puppy headed for the open door. "Well, girl, now we have a guide. I think he might take me to see your daddy again. What do you think?"

As he put the pup down, it scurried again towards the door. "Oh, no you don't. You're always looking to run out. That's why I can't take you with me tomorrow. You'd probably run into the woods and get lost."

Reese reached for the leash and called the puppy by its name for the first time. "Hey, Nitika, you little stinker. Come here. You're always running off whenever you get the chance and I'm not going to be chasing after you again."

Clipping the lead to the collar, Reese laughed as the pup tried to wrestle free. "You're getting to be a big handful, Nitika," Reese said enjoying the sound of the new name.

CHAPTER 12

"To look into the eyes of a wolf is to look into your own soul."
- Aldo Leopold, Naturalist.

Autumn returned to the Bitterroots in its unparalleled splendor of myriad colors. No gold shined more brightly than the glint of aspen leaves in brilliant sunlight, and no white could match the bark of leaning birches. Against the bluest sky, the multicolored cottonwoods and the vermilion of sumac stood forth boasting their hues, challenged only by the varying shades of the orange maples dancing in the crisp air. Spellbound and captured by its beauty, Reese stood on a granite outcrop overlooking the sparkling silver ribbon of Bass Creek meandering through a grove of bright green conifers.

Jacy glanced back at Reese who fought to keep pace. "Mister Jeff, it's not much longer. Just a little past the next hill."

"We've been hiking for hours. Let an old man catch his breath," Reese said half in jest. He was more anxious to go than to rest.

Never certain if Reese was serious, Jacy stopped and sat on his haunches peering up at Reese. "Why didn't you bring Nitika along for the hike, Mister Jeff?"

"She's a little hard to manage when she's outside. She likes to run off. I guess the wolf in her will always be there."

Jacy rose to his feet and pointed across the breathtaking expanse to a huge rock formation. The outcrop formed a bench on the painted mountainside that stretched to the limits of one's view. "See that ridge, I think that's where the pack lives."

Reese peered through his binoculars. "It's not more than an hour's hike, wouldn't you think?"

Jacy nodded and he and Reese headed for the ridge.

* * *

Two miles beyond the ridge, Dakota, Bartok and Shako led the juveniles of the pack on their first hunt. Yuma was the most anxious to go. Unlike his father Bartok, Yuma was not black and his facial mask was unusual. His sulfur-colored eyes, as if accented with eyeliner, were darkened against lighter fur and he had deep brown tear streaks running to his muzzle. It gave the juvenile a sad appearance, but belied his true nature.

Variations of color in Yuma's outer coat distinguished the young wolf from the rest of the pack. Tan, cream and white guard hair blended into grizzled golden beauty, but more compelling than his color was his attitude. His posture was always erect, tail never sagging, but held higher than his littermates' as if to flaunt his boldness and display there was little difference between him and Bartok. The wolf cub was already showing signs of becoming an alpha.

Yuma loved to play with his littermates, but the hierarchy among them was established quickly. He would often send them yelping from his overly assertive dominance. Yuma would make mock attacks on the adults, and found great delight in ambushing Dakota when he least expected it. Strangely, the only wolf he would not harass was Anoki, the old, pure white omega that lived on the fringes of the pack.

Anoki was the babysitter. It was a role she loved. Whenever the pack was off hunting, Anoki would tend to the pups. Her omega life was not easy. She was always reminded of her lowly status by the other wolves, especially her younger sister Shako. But when the pack was away, Anoki took great satisfaction in caring for the pups, and Yuma loved her. The gentle omega was beleaguered enough by the others.

Nearly black at birth, Anoki's coloration began to change as she grew older. From the beginning, her fur lightened from chocolate brown to light tan until she wore a smoky white coat. By the time she was an adult wolf, the only aberration to Anoki's snowy white pelt was a star-shaped marking in the middle of her chest beneath her neck. While Anoki stood out from her siblings and the rest of the wolves, her color became a curse for the attention she got from her pack mates. Though Anoki's coat was obviously different from the other wolves, it was the contrast of her disposition that determined the tender wolf's station within the pack. A constant target, she was tormented incessantly for that difference, and Anoki would tumble to her back whenever playful brothers and sisters would romp with her. To the other wolves it was a clear indication of capitulation, a sign of the omega wolf, and the pack took total advantage, pressing her into a role of compliance.

No wolf allowed Anoki peace. Shako enforced her dominance over the omega, especially during the mating season. If Shako detected any indication that Anoki was coming into estrous, she made certain to drive her away from the rendezvous area and keep her well beyond the vicinity of any interested male. Bartok made sure that Anoki ate last while the other wolves of the pack beset her to emulate their leader.

Dakota kindly ignored the omega; it was the impetuous Yuma who seemed to have a touch of warmth for the white wolf. He would often intervene when his littermates tormented Anoki, scrambling with them to divert their attention. But whenever Bartok, Shako or another adult displayed their authority over Anoki, Yuma could only watch. There was no way the young Yuma could intercede despite any sympathy he may have felt for the babysitter.

In early spring with the arrival of a new litter, Anoki was in her glory. She was the most excited wolf in the pack, spending her days just outside the mouth of the den fidgeting anxiously for the pups to emerge. Although she would assist the pack on every hunt during the winter, Anoki would stay behind in the warmer months to mind the pups. It was a chore she cherished and looked forward to with each birthing season. Although it seemed to be her happiest time, it marked the beginning of a season in which Anoki would suffer the most.

CHAPTER 13

"Perhaps one reason that wolves have managed to survive over the millennia is that they don't pass through nature; they become part of it."

- Scott Ian Barry, *Wolf Empire*

As summer grasses flourished, the larger ungulates the pack preyed upon regained their strength, and without the deep snows to hamper their fleetness, became much more difficult to run down. With the pack content to depend on smaller game, there was much less fare for a wolf that lagged at the den site reliant upon the pack to bring back its food. The never-ending pester of playful puppies, the many days of hunger and the occasional insult from a frustrated pack member never dimmed Anoki's spirit. As long as puppies were around, the old, white wolf was content.

Once, Yuma filched a large piece of meat away from his littermates, dragging it beyond the den area to where the temporarily banished Anoki awaited her turn to feed. It was not Yuma's intention to bring food to Anoki, his aim only to avoid sibling competition.

Knowing that Yuma was less likely to object to her presence, Anoki slipped closer to Yuma and his cache. When she was certain that Yuma was not going to object, the omega slowly began to feed on the meat that Yuma seemed willing to share.

But the ever-alert Shako spotted Yuma slinking off with the meat. When she saw that her son was allowing Anoki to eat with him, Shako reacted, scolding her sister and taking the meat from Yuma for not defending his portion of a kill from Anoki.

Yuma had ignored his mother's lessons that young get their share before older betas and omegas. But the stubbornness in Yuma was yet unbridled. Whenever he saw that Shako was preoccupied with feeding or otherwise distracted, Yuma would still, on such occasions, allow Anoki to slip away with a share of his food.

Living together as a social group, every member of Bartok's pack formed strong bonds with other pack mates. Dakota was especially fond of his nephew, Yuma. The two were inseparable, perhaps because Yuma was so much like Bartok. On his first hunt it was Dakota, not Bartok that Yuma followed.

The pack, Bartok, Shako, and three of their offspring were loping ahead of Dakota on the scent of an elk calf when Bartok slowed his pace. He caught another scent that made him stop in his tracks and turn to Dakota. Dakota immediately recognized the scent of a black bear, and realized that his brother was being cautious. With young wolves on their first hunt, Bartok did not want to risk an encounter with a formidable foe. Yuma, eager to pursue the elk scent, ran ahead, unaware of the danger his actions would bring to the pack.

Bartok and the pack quickly corralled the other juveniles as Dakota dashed after the hasty Yuma. Even with sound legs, Dakota had difficulty making up for the head start of his nephew. By the time Dakota caught up, Yuma was nearly face to face with an adult bear dragging an elk calf. The big sow bear, ready to defend its kill, stood on its hind legs gnashing and snarling rage at the two wolves. Only a few yards away from the defiant bear, Yuma made a dash for the calf. It was a critical mistake.

A vicious swat sent Yuma tumbling, the bear now in savage pursuit. Dakota charged in sinking his stubby teeth and chipped fang into the bear's lower spine, barely penetrating the thick hide. It was just enough to divert the bear and prevent it from reaching the defenseless Yuma. More infuriated than hurt, the bear spun to charge Dakota, but the wolf's quickness allowed it to stay ahead of its attacker long enough for Yuma to regain his feet and run squealing to Shako, Anoki the babysitter, and the pack.

Again running to Dakota's defense, Bartok arrived at the scene. The bear had returned to its kill, and Dakota sat panting just beyond the feeding bear. When the bear saw Bartok, it became annoyed again, and again defiance roared from the beast. Normally, Bartok would have loped away with his brother, but instead yielded to Dakota's call. Dakota yelped the sound that is the call to summon the pack. Bartok joined in. In response, Shako, the juveniles and four other pack mates appeared with cautioned steps and bristled manes.

Dakota knew that one or two wolves could not overtake an adult black bear and realized an entire pack would have difficulty trying to steal its kill. But somewhere in the absurdity of what Dakota had in mind was a lesson for the youngsters, especially Yuma.

Bartok always designated pack activity. He would dictate when to pursue prey, when to rest and where and when to travel. The alpha even decided which wolf would eat and when. Other pack members rarely influenced Bartok. But this time he deferred to his brother.

Surrounding the bear, seven adult wolves closed near as the four youngest looked on. The bear reared and roared in confrontation, trying to protect its back, as first one wolf and then another got behind it to bite at its flanks. The strategy had the bear turning from side to side, swiping at one tormentor and biting at another. The melee went on and on, but the bear would not retreat.

The wolves took turns resting in between badgering their foe until finally, after nearly an hour, the bruin began to tire. When the bear decided the elk calf was not worth defending against an onslaught eleven strong, it turned to run. Their task complete, the wolves would not pursue; they had separated the bear from the dead calf and that was all they needed to accomplish.

Yuma, either in revenge of his memorable swatting, or remiss in forgetting it, ran yelping and nipping at the heels of the bear. This time it was Bartok who ran down his son and delivered a punishing bite to his rump. Yuma turned in protest, baring his teeth. It was another act of insubordination by the young wolf that turned into a painful lesson. Bartok, furious for the disobedience, clamped powerful jaws on Yuma's neck and flipped him over onto his back. Grasping Yuma's muzzle in his mouth, the big alpha male asserted his dominance, holding the young wolf down. Several seconds passed before Yuma calmed enough for Bartok to release his hold.

Yuma maintained a prolonged glare into his father's eyes. It was not the first time the young wolf had displayed the behavior typical of an alpha. Bartok snarled at Yuma until he turned away. It was schooling for the youngster, but he still had a lot more to learn.

The pack turned its attention to the kill it had stolen. All eyes were on Bartok as he began to feed. No wolf would begin to eat until the alpha became indulged with his choice part of the carcass. One by one, pack members were allowed to feed in the order of their status within the pack. Shako and Dakota were the first to get Bartok's permission, followed by the other betas. The omega wolf, Anoki, always the last to feed, was surprised to be given Bartok's permission before Yuma was allowed to approach. Bartok, still not pleased with Yuma's behavior, made his son grovel for a share of the meat.

CHAPTER 14

"The howl of a wolf. One of the most beautiful animal noises."
- Gerald Durell, *Beasts in My Belfry*

By the time the pack had consumed half the remains of the yearling elk, Reese and Jacy, alerted by the sounds of the entire ordeal, had gotten close enough to witness the outcome. Lying on their stomachs several hundred yards downwind of the preoccupied wolves, they watched the pack consume what was left of the carcass. It was the first time either Jacy Cayuse or Jeffrey Reese had seen wolves interacting, living in the wild.

Reese held his binoculars on the wolves and whispered to Jacy. "I never thought I'd get to see this. Wolves are really back in the Bitterroots. I mean wild wolves, wolves that were born here. This is awesome."

When Jacy didn't answer, Reese looked over his shoulder to see the young Indian gasp for air in an attempt to stifle his emotions. Reese hesitated for his own pulse to calm and then handed his binoculars to Jacy. Jeffrey Reese knew what the boy was feeling. He knew what every Native American would feel if he could behold what Jacy was seeing. The wolf and the Indian shared similar fates in their histories, Reese thought – both shamefully held in low esteem.

Toward evening of Reese's most cherished day since his wolf project began, he watched the sated black wolf rise from his feeding and stretch. The other wolves, one by one, aped their leader and Reese knew they would all soon follow the ebony alpha away.

Jacy nudged the binoculars toward Reese, but he refused them. "No, Jay, you use them."

"Mister Jeff, I want you to see something," Jacy whispered as he insisted by pushing the binoculars toward Reese. "See the black lobo? He was the one with the wolf I caught. Look at the one next to him. The big one. I think he's Nitika's father. Look, look!"

Reese took the binoculars and once again looked upon the wolf he had nursed back to the wild. He recognized the animal as the mate to his Gretchen, the sire of her only offspring Nitika.

The choking lump deep behind his tongue almost made it impossible for him to answer. "Yes, I think it is." Reese swallowed the lingering thickness in his throat. "It definitely is," he said softly.

* * *

The boy and the man watched as the pack began to stir. Caught in a moment of joy for their success, Bartok was the first to bay, followed by Dakota and Shako. The deep, resonant voices of the adult wolves harmonized with the higher-toned youngsters and a sound as mellifluous as any concert rang out. The song flowed through the hollows, echoed off rock ledges and seemed to linger in the valley before joining chorus with the soft whistling of an evening breeze to disperse over the tops of giant hemlocks and fade into the sleepy silence of twilight.

Its joy having been sung out into the dusk of the Bitterroots, the wolf family gathered, licking and nuzzling in a display of genuine affection and delight, nudging and sidling up to one another. Then, they grouped together and milled about as if waiting for a signal before forming an ordered file to follow Bartok.

Like a variegated, furred train on tracks too distant to see, Reese watched the pack wend the invisible rails into the fading light. Bartok, the powerful black engine leading the way, was the first to disappear from view, while Anoki, the little white caboose, was the last wolf to chug off into the distance.

* * *

Darkness closed in as Reese and Jacy made their way home. The clarity of the night air allowed a trillion stars to light the way as Jacy found the same unmarked paths he had taken before.

During an hour's walk in complete silence, Reese thought about Elizabeth English. He could not shake the notion that she would love to have been there to see the wolves. Mesmerized, Reese could hear her soft laughter, he could see her eyes widen as she watched the animals and he could feel her excitement. For the first time since meeting Elizabeth he thought about how her reaction might measure to Samantha's and he was not convinced that Elizabeth's enthusiasm would have been less by comparison.

The scars of past memories were beginning to dissolve.

Jacy's voice broke the spell. "Mister Jeff, did you see the cub what was different colored from the rest?"

"I did see one that was lighter than the others. Kind of yellowish."

"I could see 'em in the binoculars. He was one of the young ones. Real pretty fur. Like gold. He was the one what ate last."

"I noticed that. He must be an omega."

"I don't think he's an omega, he's only a cub. He shoulda ate with the other cubs."

"You're right about that," Reese said furrowing his brow.

Jacy simpered proudly. "I could see his face real good. He looked sad, but I liked him best in the pack 'cause he was golden. Which lobo did you like?"

"I guess if I had to pick a favorite," said Reese, "it would be the one that's Nitika's papa."

Jacy stopped walking. "What do you think Nitika will look like when she gets big?"

"She's already looking more like a wolf than a German shepherd. I think she's going to resemble her father," came the sad answer.

"I hope so!" the boy said.

Reese merely smiled at the youth's unintended insensitivity. He knew that Jacy loved wolves more than anything else.

CHAPTER 15

"You may feed the wolf as much as you like. He will always glance toward the door."

- Russian Proverb

While Reese's encounter with the wolves energized him, his subconscious continued to generate the bad dreams that worked to deny him of refreshing sleep. In some dreams he'd see Elizabeth English. He'd try to go to her, but faceless women and dogs resembling wolves got in his way. He'd push and shove toward Elizabeth, but the colorless wolf-like dogs tripped him and he'd become entangled within the snarl of animals.

Tiring, he'd fight to get free, but he'd stumble and fall into the menagerie before he could reach her. Struggling, he would try to get up, but exhaustion weakened him and he'd fail again to get to Elizabeth. The same dreams recurred nearly every night, with the same ending. Samantha was always trying to return, but she'd never arrive. He'd try to get to Elizabeth, but could not reach her.

Though the nightmares persisted, Reese used the wakeful hours for work, the only advantage to his bouts with insomnia. Within a few weeks he was able to complete his portion of the documentary *The National Graphic* had sent him to Montana to do, and he called his editor.

"Hello Dave, how are you?"

David Hornman bellowed into the phone. "Well, what do you

know? If it isn't the wolf man! So, I understand you finished our story."

"I'm sending you everything I've got. You should have it tonight."

"Good, good. Listen, we're sending the photo crew up there. They should meet you in a few days to complete the project. Now you're sure they'll have some beasties to film, or were they figments of that imagination of yours?"

"No, real wolves, Dave, not beasts. They're great animals. Real honest to goodness gray wolves, living back where they belong."

"Don't get so sappy. I read your stuff about that wolf you had. It's going to make a nice piece to go with the feature. Fair job," Hornman teased. Then he changed the subject. "So, now that your part is done, are you ready to show photographers around and then get back to Chicago?"

"I don't know. I don't know if I want to come back yet. Besides, I'm not going back in the field any time soon."

Though Hornman knew that Reese was more serious minded and seldom dug into the teasing banter the editor so often used, he was not certain that Reese wasn't putting him on. "What the hell are you talking about, Jeff?" Hornman croaked.

"I need some time. I was thinking of taking a leave from the job. Maybe do some freelance work. This wolf thing really got under my skin. I don't know; I was thinking maybe I'd write a novel. Something about wolves, perhaps."

"Who's going to show the photo boys these wolves you found?"

Reese laughed to himself ignoring the insensitivity. "Just tell them to come. And, by the way, you needn't worry. I'll introduce them to a good guide. A Nez Perce kid. He knows the area and the wolves a heck of a lot better than I do."

"An Injun? Jeff, this is too important to leave to some Indian kid!"

Reese laughed into the phone. "Horny, you just gave me an idea. Maybe I'll devote a few chapters of my book to Indians. I don't know which is more misunderstood, the Indian or the timber wolf."

"You'd better get back here to your desk as soon as possible Wolfie. The woods are starting to get to you."

"I'm serious, Dave. I'm thinking of spending the winter here after the photographers leave. If the boss doesn't approve the rent for the cabin, I'll take it on myself."

There was a long silence before Hornman spoke. "You *are* serious about this, aren't you?"

"Do you want me to talk to the boss, or will you do it for me?"

There was a somber tone to Hornman's reply. "I think the magazine will foot the rent, but I'm not so sure the old man is going to be too happy to lose his outdoor writer for any length of time. How long were you thinking about?"

Reese clenched his teeth before answering. "Year, maybe two at the most." Then he hurried into a negotiation before Hornman could respond. "Look, I don't have to be at my desk to write for the *Graphic*. This is the age of technology, isn't it? I have my computer. I want you to make it happen for me, Dave. What do you say?"

There was another long pause before Hornman answered. "I'll talk to him, but damn, whose shoes will I bust if you're up in the sticks?"

"The age of technology, remember? Email me. And don't forget. We'll need some extra money to pay the guide."

* * *

Reese continued to regret denying Elizabeth. Whenever she entered his mind, however, he found himself looking for diversion. While waiting for Hornman's answer, he spent the next few days working with Nitika. He spent as much time as he could with her to occupy himself and distract thoughts about Elizabeth.

He had dogs before Gretchen, but none were as strong-headed as Nitika, especially when she was outdoors. It was nearly impossible not to keep her tethered. When she got loose, she ran and her fearlessness got her into trouble. Once, Reese had to employ pliers to remove porcupine quills, and another time it took several tomato juice, lemon oil and baking soda baths before he could tolerate her after a skunk encounter.

Nitika was large for her age. She had oversized feet and stubby ears. Long, dark-gray fur had replaced her downy coat, and a black roan saddle was the only resemblance she bore to her mother. Reese did not like to keep the animal tied. As a pup, he could always run her down when she sprinted off, but the older she got, the more difficult that became. Her legs were long, like a wolf's, and she loved to use them.

Jacy liked to be around Nitika and came by the cabin to play with her. Now that he was a constant visitor, Reese would allow him to take Nitika outdoors. The young Indian had no problem running after her and he loved to take her into the woods. The two would be gone for hours, and Jacy would return with excited chitchat.

"Mister Jeff, Nitika isn't afraid of anything. She runs after everything! She chased a bobcat bigger 'n her."

"Yeah, I noticed she even tried to attack your horse this morning."

"Oh, you see that? I'll leave ol' Buckskin down the road next time so Nitika won't scare 'im."

Reese chuckled. "I guess that might work, but I think she's got a lopsided mixture of traits. She seems to have more genes from her ancient past than from the fifteen thousand years of domesticity."

Jacy's quizzical look made Reese simplify. "She takes after her father more than her mother."

"I like that about her," Jacy said.

Reese smiled.

* * *

The next morning a call came early. When Reese answered the phone, David Hornman skipped his hello and went right into good-natured banter. "You know something wolf man, you should thank your stars you've got me here to do your dirty work. Do you know how long it took me to convince the boss to let you do what you want?"

"I'll bite. How long?"

"Less than a minute. Old man Thornton said he's glad to be rid of you."

"That long, huh?"

"Yup," said Hornman. Then he paused for effect. "Oh! Wow! I almost forgot to tell you, Wolfie. I asked him for some time off, too. I'm going to write my own novel dedicated to you. I'm calling it The Abduction of Sanity by a Pack of Wolves. Thornton says he'll pay me a million for it."

Reese laughed. "How generous of him. Did he throw in money for the kid, or did you forget to mention the guide?"

Hornman loved to nettle. "How could I negotiate for him? You never told me how many beads and arrows he needs or the size of his moccasins. Besides, we're all out of wampum. We spent it on a big teepee for you to live in while you're up there."

"You're a regular riot, Dave. Maybe you should get your own show. I know you didn't forget to ask, or you wouldn't be pulling my leg."

"No, I didn't forget. Your Indian will get paid. The boss says that'll be included in the photo guys' expense money for as long as they'll need to use him."

"You did good, Horny. I'm proud of you."

"Yeah, yeah," Hornman clucked. "Look, the crew is grabbing a charter out of O'Hare early tomorrow morning. They'll rent a van and meet you in Stevensville around noon, so don't get lost in the woods. You've got to be there when they call."

"I'll try to stay local."

Reese rushed his goodbyes. Nitika was scratching wildly at the cabin door to be let out. Reese hurried to save what remained of the woodwork floor moldings already worn from her scratching.

"Hey, you little rascal. You're going to wreck this place. I can't keep up with you," Reese said grabbing the leash off its hook in his sprint to the door.

Outside, Reese strained against the leash; Nitika tugged with most of her might to break free. The animal had more spirit than he could manage, and he felt bad that he had to keep it tied. Reese always held hope that Nitika would be more like Gretchen than her mate, more like a dog than a wolf, but he knew the truth.

For an instant, the words stalled in his throat. "You want to run, don't you?"

As if she understood, Nitika relaxed her pull against the lead, sat on her haunches and threw back her head. Reese stood spellbound as small yelps, momentarily trapped, rattled free. The sound melted into a disjointed squeal before ringing forth from her muzzle into a feeble, high-pitched yowl. It sent a cool shiver up Reese's spine stiffening the hair on the back of his neck.

Kneeling, the man tugged gently at the leash and the animal came to him. Nitika was never comfortable being held, so Reese suppressed his urge to hug her as he would Gretchen. Instead, he stroked the side of her face, rubbed her ears and spoke gently.

"Nitika, you're going to have a much better life when this project is finished. I promise."

Nitika cocked her head as Reese continued. "I'm not going to be able to stay here forever, and Chicago is no place for a ---," Reese swallowed hard before saying, "wolf."

CHAPTER 16

"Inescapably, the realization was being borne in upon my preconditioned mind that the centuries-old and universally accepted human concept of wolf character was a palpable lie."
- Farley Mowat, *Never Cry Wolf*

Although he had thought about her many times, Reese didn't call Elizabeth. During the hours waiting for Jacy, Reese needed something pleasant to occupy his mind. Thinking about Elizabeth English gave him the resolve he needed to go through with his plan.

He glanced at Nitika and spoke to her as he had to Gretchen. "Nitika, do you think I should call her? I kind of miss --- not talking to her. She's probably angry that I ignored her so long. What do you think?"

Reese was expecting Nitika to sit up and pay attention like Gretchen would, but the pup lay curled by the front door with her nose pressed against the frame sniffing at the outside world.

Reese chuckled to himself as Nitika ignored him. "You're no help, Nitika. Why do I even talk to you?"

When Jacy finally got to the cabin, Reese sat him down and pulled a chair close to him. "I want to talk to you about something, Jay."

The boy squirmed at Reese's sober tone and glanced around the room looking for Nitika. "Is something wrong with Nitika?"

"No. I just tied her out back for a while," Reese said. "She's got a bone bigger than she is to keep her busy. I wanted to speak with you before you walk her. I've arranged a little job for you as a guide for some photographers. I'd like you to take them back up into the Bass Creek area."

Except for a deep breath of relief, Jacy was silent. Despite his fondness for Jeff Reese, the young Indian could not help being nervous around adults, especially white men when they became serious.

Reese tapped a hand on Jacy's shoulder. "It's a chance for you to make a few dollars."

A curious frown crept into Jacy's face, but didn't hold. "Mister Jeff, aren't you gonna go, too?"

"No, Jay. I'm going to stay here and look after Nitika until you finish. You may have to camp out up there a few days or even a week so they can get pictures of the wolf pack. I can't leave Nitika for that length of time. Who'd watch her?"

Jacy shrugged. "Nobody, I guess."

"You see, Jay, that's a problem I've been thinking about for a while now. I need someone who'll be able to manage her when she gets older. Someone responsible who could take her and provide a good home."

Reese noticed the boy's shoulders droop. "Jay, do you know of anyone?"

Jacy gazed toward the back door and swallowed hard before mustering a weak reply. "No sir, Mister Jeff. I don't know nobody."

"Well, don't worry. I think I do. I found this fella who might be willing to take her."

Shaking his head slowly without moving eyes that bore into Reese, Jacy stepped back, his voice nearly inaudible. "Who?" he asked.

"There's this guy who'd be perfect. If you don't know anyone, I'll ask him."

As if quelling an itch, Jacy rubbed a knuckle into his palm. "But, if you give her away, I won't get to see her."

"I know you two have grown pretty close, but you'll have plenty of time for Nitika. In fact, you'll have more time with her than anyone."

Jacy scrunched up his brow and searched Jeff Reese's eyes.

"What do you mean?"

"I mean you're the person I'm going to give her to. I want you to have Nitika…that's if it's okay with you."

Jacy's jaw slackened. "If it's okay with me? It's okay with me, yeah it's okay with me."

"So, is that a yes?"

"Oh, yes, Mister Jeff. For sure it is. For sure!"

Reese thought he saw tears well up in the boy's eyes. "You're not going soft on me now are you Jay?"

"No Mister Jeff. Nez Perce men never cry. Even if somebody dies."

Reese recalled that Jacy had told him that once before, so he turned his head and looked away to help the proud Indian keep his claim.

Jacy rocked back and forth for several minutes. He didn't speak.

He didn't need to.

* * *

Winters come early in the Bitterroots. At the onset of the first significant snowfall, Jacy led the photography crew out of the basin where they had successfully photographed Bartok's pack. Nine days had passed since they left for the Bass Creek area, and the men, anxious to get home, packed their gear and left to catch the nine o'clock flight back to O'Hare.

His heart racing with anticipation, Jacy jumped on his snowmobile and sped for Reese's cabin. Forgetting goggles or a facemask, the sting of frigid wind whipping at Jacy's face froze the boy's smile. Even with the throttle opened to the max, the vehicle moved slower than Jacy wanted.

Reese had already prepared a few things for Jacy to take with him when he came for Nitika. Gretchen's leash was the first thing Reese handed the boy when he arrived.

"I'm not sure you'll be able to use this much, but I won't be needing it anymore."

Jacy took the lead and fingered its soft, braided leather. Kneeling to attach it to Nitika's collar, he looked up at Reese and dropped his glance when their eyes met. He didn't speak, and Reese was thankful for that. Then the boy tucked the watering bowl and food dish under his arm and Nitika dragged him towards the door.

Outside, Jacy struggled to restrain the anxious animal. He then turned to face Reese. His voice cracked as he called out. "Mister Jeff. I'm gonna take good care of her."

"I'm sure of that, Jay. I know you will."

Although he was curious, Reese didn't watch to see how Jacy managed with Nitika and the snowmobile. The quick whirring of the machine driving off told him the boy had everything under control, and it made Reese feel confident.

Reese knew he'd be sad without Gretchen, but he felt certain that keeping Nitika would hold no consolation. As he thought about the coming months of his life, a feeling of loneliness gripped tightly and pulled him to his desk. He sat and reached for a drawer that he rarely opened. There, he fingered through old greeting cards, frayed letters and nostalgic photographs. He found a picture of Samantha that he had forgotten about and gazed at the snapshot. Intrigued by a strange sensation, he stared more intently. He thought he saw in her face a look that seemed different from the one he remembered from the last time he held the photo. He turned the picture over and read: "Life is good, my love, and it will even get better, Sam."

Reese felt an aura of warmth as he turned the photo again to look at the beautiful face and spoke to it. "I miss you so much Sammy. What'll I do?"

Samantha seemed to answer as Reese imagined her smile growing broader when he suddenly remembered Elizabeth's note. He returned the photo to the drawer, searched his desk and found the envelope.

Reese felt still more warmth as he thought about Elizabeth. He wondered if she would be receptive to a call after he had ignored her for so long. With the scars of past memories fading, he picked up his phone to dial, but stopped. Instead, he turned to his computer and brushed his fingertips over the keyboard that had given him his greatest comfort since Samantha and Gretchen. He thought about his life and he felt more convinced than ever that he was about to make the right decisions.

With a single finger he casually pecked at the keys typing subconsciously. Characters and spaces appeared. There before him, the title of his first novel: Cry Wolf, Cry.

CHAPTER 17

"If we push wolves into a dead-end place of no-mystery, no-wildness, we will follow."

- Rick Bass, *The Ninemile Wolves*

Elizabeth English picked up her ringing cellular and was shocked to hear Reese's voice. She had to clutch the phone with both trembling hands to keep it from falling. She felt the sway of adrenal fluid waltz through her bloodstream thumping warmness into her chest as her heart danced more rapidly. It took a moment, that timeless pause that stops the breath, for Elizabeth to gain her composure, but finally she was able to speak. "Hi Jeff," she said as if no time had passed since she last spoke to him. "Are you feeling better?"

Jeff felt a knot in his vocal cords tighten as he spoke. "I'm doing pretty well," he said trying to swallow the bond in his throat. "I know you'll find this difficult to believe, but I've wanted to call you for weeks. I've been having a difficult time admitting things to myself."

Still shaking, Elizabeth flicked her hair away from her ear so she could hear him better. "No. Don't think about it. I'm glad you called. Are we okay?"

"You're okay. You've always been okay. I'm the one who wasn't. But I'm happy I finally called."

Elizabeth felt her pulse become more normal. "I'm happy, too, Jeff."

"I've got a lot to tell you about if you're willing to listen."

"I've got time, but if you're looking for an agenda…" she paused a moment, then laughed.

Reese, too, became more relaxed and laughed with her, and before an awkward silence could interrupt his frame of mind, he got to the main reason for his call. "Beth, I'd like to see you."

Her voice sounded sweeter than he could have hoped it would. "I'd like to see you, too."

Reese suggested they meet at a halfway point, but she insisted on driving to his cabin. When he hung up, Reese was relieved. Subconsciously, allowing another woman into his life was a betrayal. Now that he had acted on his attraction to Elizabeth, he was finally confronting a persisting anxiety, and he felt a leaden shawl of guilt lift from his shoulders.

* * *

It was late evening when Elizabeth arrived. A fierce, cold wind howled under the eaves of the cabin and a flaring fire crackled and popped in the oversized, fieldstone fireplace of the modest log house. Reese had been pacing when he saw the headlights of Elizabeth's SUV bounce up the rutted driveway. Before she could get out of the vehicle, Reese jogged out into the frigid night to greet her.

Elizabeth stepped from the car and opened her arms to an embrace that lingered, neither wanting to interrupt the tender hug. Standing on tiptoes, she stretched to nestle her cheek against Reese's neck, the tip of her cold nose brushed his ear and she whispered. "You've got no coat on. It's supposed to snow. You'll catch cold out here."

"Don't have one. I've been meaning to buy a new one. Just haven't gotten around to it," Reese said as he took Elizabeth's hand and led her inside. "Care for a drink? I made us some chili, so you may need one."

"Good chili has to be spicy," she said.

"I wasn't worried about the spice. I was hoping the drink would disguise my cooking."

"I'll bet it's good. But I'll drink whatever you're having."

The couple sat near the fire, shared chili, wine and conversation.

Pausing only to put more wood on the fire, Reese did most of the talking. The hours passed quickly as he told Elizabeth about Samantha, Jacy, Nitika and his plans to write a novel.

Realizing that he was dominating much of the conversation, Reese changed the subject. “Tell me about your family.”

Elizabeth suddenly began to fidget. She glanced around the room looking for a clock. “Gee, what time is it?”

Reese got up to check. Neither he nor Elizabeth had been paying attention to the time and it was after midnight when they looked outside. A steady snowfall had blanketed the driveway and the wind drifted snow up to the doors of Elizabeth’s Chevy Blazer.

“I’ll feel better if you’ll let me drive you home;” Reese said, “the weather is really nasty.”

“I’m not going to risk either one of us driving in this. I’ll camp here if it’s all right with you.”

It was the most logical choice, and Reese was pleased the suggestion to stay was hers. “Sure, you’re more than welcome. You take my room. I’ll be fine right here by the fire.”

“Let’s not worry about that right now,” she said. “Do you have coffee?”

“Sure, I’ll make some,” he said as he headed for a cupboard, “but will your folks be worried? Do you need to make a call?”

Elizabeth followed Reese into the kitchen and stood beside him. “It’s only my father. He’s not well and retires early. It’s a big house and he won’t miss me until late tomorrow morning when he gets up. I’ll call him then.”

“Only you and your father? Small family.”

“I have a brother somewhere. He ran off years ago. Lord knows where he is.”

Elizabeth’s eyes searched the kitchen and came to rest on her own hands toying with an empty wine glass. “Mom left, too,” she sighed. “She had a problem dealing with dad’s drinking. My father is a tough man to live with, Jeff.”

Reese noticed uneasiness when she spoke about her family so he tried to divert her attention. “Hey, I make a terrible cup of coffee. Can you give me a hand?”

Elizabeth brightened. “You said that about the chili and it was great.”

"Chili's easy. Coffee's an art. I need some help here."

"Okay, but only if you tell me more about yourself."

Reese handed her the coffee tin, "No. No more about me. How come you're not with a guy? How is it that you're not married by now?"

Elizabeth responded to Reese's broad smile with one of her own. "Are you suggesting I'm old enough?"

"No, but eligible enough. You've got a lot to offer."

"I've never found anyone I'd like to be with."

Reese shook his head. "Not even a childhood sweetheart? Not even puppy love?"

"Puppy love. Yes. I would have loved a puppy, but J D doesn't like dogs. He thinks they're bad to have around cattle."

"Too much like wolves?" he said and ducked a half-hearted punch. "Your father sure made you miss out. There's nothing quite like having a good dog in your life."

"To tell you the truth, he wasn't too crazy for any of the men around here, either. He probably would have been disappointed if I dated a rancher, and having been a rancher's daughter, I'm not so sure I'd like that life anyway."

"Oh, I don't know. It sure is beautiful country out here."

"It's not the country I'm talking about," she said.

Reese thought he sensed a slight annoyance in her. Not wanting to irritate with another question, he said: "With your looks and smarts you can have any lifestyle you want."

Elizabeth stood measuring out spoonfuls of ground coffee. She stopped and turned to face Reese. "Do you like my looks?" she asked, posing the question more seriously than Reese thought she should have.

"Are you kidding? You are kidding, right?"

She didn't answer. She just flashed that smile he hated to see fade from her face.

Reese could not look away from her eyes. "I love your looks," he whispered. "They take my mind away."

Stepping closer to Reese, Elizabeth remained serious. "I like your looks," she whispered back, "I also like you, too. An awful lot."

The warmth of her words radiated through his chest like a shot of brandy on a February day. They stood in silence for a moment studying the color of each other's eyes. For an instant Reese got lost trying to decide where the soft brown of the iris turned to hazel. He understood why he wrestled with which of her features was her most attractive, but he could not understand being without a preference. Her eyes, he decided, were his favorite.

"This may seem insignificant to you," she said, "but I just couldn't stand being ignored by you all that time."

Her eyes glistened as they searched his face, and Reese felt their sadness soak into his heart. He so much wanted to see Elizabeth's eyes laugh again. "Maybe I tried a little too hard to ignore you like I did. I was just afraid to complicate matters."

For an instant, he thought of trying to explain the vagaries he fought in his mind with regard to his love for Samantha, but he decided to avoid what he, himself, found difficult to understand.

"This wolf thing," he said shaking his head and gazing downward, "it's like an obsession for me to see those animals vindicated. I know it's not your choice, but the world you live in and everything in it is in complete contrast to what I believe."

"I understand," she said, "but you should understand something, too. You're important to me. I'm beginning to --"

Reese put his hand up and touched his fingertips to her lips before she could finish her thought. The slight quaver in her voice and the absence of a smile told him she might say something more serious than he wanted to hear. Reese was still reluctant to revisit desires he thought dormant.

Before he could take his hand away, she grabbed and held it to her lips. She did not kiss his fingers, but for a moment, held them to her mouth with gentle pressure that seemed to flow a warm current into his hand. When she released her grip, the faint sensation subsided and he was unsettled. Only Samantha's touch had ever made that happen, and he was afraid to think it was something more than imagination.

"Did you feel that?" she asked.

He was as surprised as she, but would not admit that it was anything but static. Standing on a wooden floor, his explanation was weak, but she accepted it.

They drank coffee and talked until dawn before deciding to retire. Elizabeth said goodnight and went to Reese's room leaving him trying to reconcile the revived feeling he had in the pit of his stomach. It felt as if a loveable puppy about the size of a gumdrop had crawled inside him. He felt it circle around, turn and circle again until it became warm and comfortable and then it settled in his chest, where it nuzzled his heart and slowly began to thaw it.

CHAPTER 18

"If we understood the prey's advantages we would have greater sympathy for the predator as being the hapless link in its ecosystem."
- Chris McBride, *The White Lions of Timbavati*

When the Rocky Mountain autumn ended and snow began to deepen, the hunting strategies of Bartok's wolf pack changed. The pack, free from bothersome insects and the burden of trying to keep cool, became more active by day. With the oppressive heat and the annoying summer molt behind it, the pack became more invigorated and willing to travel greater distances in search of prey. The kind of prey the wolves sought dictated the way they hunted.

With the freeze came the lack of forage for the larger animals that wolves preyed upon. As the snow and ice accumulated, some deer, moose and elk began to weaken, making them more vulnerable. The deep snow hampered the escape of bighorn sheep and mountain goats. The coldest season was friendlier to Bartok and his pack than to their quarry. Winter, the time of the wolf, was upon the land.

Yuma was into his second winter when Bartok's wolves turned their attention to the elk and moose, their favored fare. Never wanting to follow, Yuma was always in the mix of the chase toward the head of the pack. Only Bartok and Dakota would be in the lead with Yuma close behind. Even Shako would trail her powerful son as he plowed through snowdrifts like the prow of an ice cutter, his narrow chest slicing a wake for his mother to follow. Yuma's aggressiveness made him a capable hunter, but in certain instances that aggressiveness became reckless.

Usually the wolves would watch the elk for as long as it took them to spot a weakness. A limp, a gaunt torso, a sagging head were signs of susceptibility and were eyed with interest. When a potential target was chosen, the pack would disperse and surround it in an attempt to separate a particular elk from the herd. Yuma, though, had ideas of his own. No elk or moose was too big for him even if it showed no vulnerability. To the young wolf, the bigger the prey, the more meat for the pack, but this abandon was about to become a tactic that Yuma would forever regret.

During a chase-and-watch, a tremendous bull veered from the elk herd and headed for a windblown hillside beneath an umbrella of conifers. There, the snow was only inches deep and afforded the elk an advantage. In deeper snow the heavy bull would sink to its belly and be unable to use one of its more formidable defenses, flailing hooves.

The pack, except for Yuma, Shako and Anoki, continued to dog the herd and paid no attention to the powerful elk that knew its best chances lay where snow was shallowest. With Yuma leading the way, his mother and Anoki approached the bull that was now standing defiantly in an area that afforded the big animal an optimum advantage against the three wolves that surrounded it.

A single male wolf the size of Bartok might overtake and kill a cow elk, but a nine-hundred-pound bull with a spectacular rack of lance-like antlers was a task for the entire pack, not two female wolves led by an impulsive youth.

Watching its every move the threesome kept circling the elk waiting for an opportunity. An hour passed and Shako glanced over her shoulder. With less than the pack's full complement, she knew the large bull was a dangerous animal to attack and she wanted more help. With Yuma facing the massive antlers, Anoki slipped to the rear of the great animal, but did not get too close. Her experience told her that bulls are easier to attack from behind, but she knew that was only possible when the animal was fleeing or bogged in deep snow.

The shadows from the huge hemlock under which the elk stood began to lengthen with the waning day. Neither the wolves nor the elk moved and the standoff continued. As long as the wolves made no attempt to attack, and the elk could keep them in sight, the bull was content with the stalemate. It would stand for hours if it had to. The elk had much more to be patient about than the hungry wolves and the big animal sensed it.

Without a sign to indicate the pack would return, Shako became restless. The matriarch knew that an attempt on the elk would be futile and she began to pace. In an instant, as the bull turned its attention to Shako's movement, Yuma seized an opportunity and sprang. With agility, the wolf vaulted onto the elk's back and bit viciously into its withers. Shocked, the bull threw back its head and spun frantically. The large antlers nearly speared Yuma as the elk swept them across its back to separate the wolf from its hold.

With the elk's head thrusting back at Yuma, Shako's leap was lightning fast as she struck at the animal's exposed throat and took a fierce hold. In panic, the elk swung its body savagely in circles sending Yuma sprawling fifteen feet through the air, but it could not dislodge Shako's fangs.

Now Anoki sprung into the attack. She attempted a lunge at the bull's underbelly, but the superior weight and strength of the elk broke her hold and Anoki, too, was cast aside. Regaining his feet, Yuma made another leap for the elk's back. This time he mounted the bull farther back on its rump, away from the slashing horn and bit deeply.

The sting of Yuma's bite to its spine had the elk jumping and kicking with all of its strength, something it would not have been able to do in deeper snow. Again, Yuma was thrown from the animal's back and Shako, too, was tossed aside and nearly trampled.

This time, luck was on the side of the prey. Had Shako's bite been a few centimeters closer to the center of the throat, her fangs would have penetrated the jugular and the skirmish might have been over. But it raged on with neither side gaining an advantage.

Shako and Anoki knew that even though the snow was not deep enough to restrict it, more wolves in the fight would have sealed the bull's fate. Although it could take hours, they knew that help from the pack would have tired the elk as the wolves would spell each other with rest. Now, all four combatants began to tire, prolonging the ordeal in favor of the elk.

After a short breather, the three wolves gathered themselves, but so did the elk. It was Anoki that made the mistake. She perceived an opening and sprang. Although the bull was bleeding, its injuries were not serious and it was still able to defend itself as it flailed its hooves at the charging wolf. A sledgehammer kick from a back hoof caught the white wolf squarely on the star-like spot of its chest below the throat, slamming the animal into the trunk of the towering hemlock. The force of the kick was so great that Anoki fell unconscious onto the snow, blood trickling from her nose and mouth. The fight was over.

Shako went to the fallen wolf's side and nudged her, licking the blood from Anoki's mouth and nostrils. Yuma crept up to Shako's side. He had never seen his mother concerned for Anoki before, and he was puzzled by what he saw as affection.

It was one of the only times the alpha female seemed to show kind attention to her sister. Shako never disliked Anoki; it was Anoki's fate to be an omega, her place in the world of the wolf.

Yuma always saw affection displayed between pack-mates. Puppies received the most, and returning absentees got their share, but hardly ever an omega. When Yuma saw Shako paw and nuzzle Anoki, he was seeing something new to his young lupine world. The affectionate display was sincere, and Anoki would have felt privileged by Shako's warmth, but the omega never enjoyed the rarity.

The pack's loyal babysitter, the gentle, old white wolf was dead.

Anoki lay in the muddy debris-strewn snow. Shako whimpered and Yuma stood silently staring at Anoki. Minutes passed before Yuma could turn his head from the dreadful scene. When he did, the bull elk was gone. Although Yuma could not reason that attacking the elk was poor judgment, he would never forget the incident, and for the remainder of his life the experience was a part of his world.

CHAPTER 19

"These animals, who have been maligned for centuries, despised as the embodiment of all that is cowardly, savage and cruel, clearly care for one another and show signs of what I would call nothing less than empathy and compassion."

- Jim Dutcher, *Wolves at Our Door*

The Nez Perce land was a good place for Nitika to grow up, but Jacy soon realized the animal was not as obedient as he had hoped it would be. Neighbors constantly complained about the mysterious thefts of venison jerky from their drying-racks. Nitika's mischievous temperament and constant harassment of all other pets in the vicinity earned her the epithet the stalking *shon tonga.*

As she grew older, Jacy would take Nitika into the wild whenever possible. It was where she seemed most comfortable, but as months passed it became more difficult for the boy to get her to return home. More than once she wandered farther than Jacy had planned and he became hoarse in his attempts to call her. On one occasion, Nitika's roaming had Jacy spending an entire night in the forest before he could get her to come back to him.

Nitika had assumed the role of a loner, running off for hours at a time whenever she wasn't tethered. Jacy, resigned to his diminishing closeness to Nitika, realized that it wouldn't be long before the animal's urge to run took it farther into the surrounding mountains. He knew it would only be a matter of time before she would leave permanently. He wanted to release her and thought about it constantly, but wondered how Reese would react if Nitika got lost in the wilderness.

The boy called Jeff Reese. "Hello Mister Jeff, it's Jacy."

"Well, hello there Jay. How are you?"

"I'm okay," Jacy said, but the tone in his voice and a long pause told otherwise.

"You're calling about Nitika aren't you?" Reese asked trying to ease the boy's apparent discomfort.

"How did you know, Mister Jeff?"

"You're not the only one in these parts who knows a little something about wolves. Unless she got hurt or someone killed her, you're calling to tell me she ran away."

"No, Mister Jeff. She's okay. She's here. I can't keep her tied. I'm scared she's gonna get lost."

"She can't get lost from where she wants to be, Jay. Her nose won't let her."

"Do ya think she kin live all alone in the hills?"

"If she runs off and discovers that she can't make it, then she'll probably come back to you. But you already know that, don't you?"

Reese knew the chances of survival for a hybrid like Nitika were nearly impossible in the wild, but he also knew that she was strong-willed and tough enough to press the improbable odds.

Reese knew exactly what Jacy wanted to do. "Why don't you just let her free? Untie her. You and Nitika will both be happier."

Jacy was stunned by the intuitive remark. "I was thinkin' 'bout that," he said.

That evening, Jacy took Nitika for a long hike back into the flinty hills not far from Bass Creek, removed her collar and with a final stroke of her magnificent coat, let her run. After she was well out of sight, the boy called. "Nitikaaaah. Nitikaaaah. Nitikaaaah." He did not expect her to respond. His calls were more for his benefit than for hers.

Nitika was alone. She had wandered too far to return before nightfall, but, characteristically, she was unafraid. Nitika felt an intuitive calling, something beyond her association with man, and she followed it. She was obeying an inbred urge, more from the genes of her wild father than from those of her domestic mother. Nitika heard Jacy's distant calls just as she had heard them before, but chose to ignore them and ran farther into the night.

CHAPTER 20

"As we become more intimate with these beings, we gain a better understanding of our own role in the circle of life."
- Rob Edward, Director
Sinapu Carnivore Restoration Program

Reese was working on his book. Now that he had allowed himself to feel comfortable with Elizabeth, he was able to concentrate more easily and found the challenge of writing a novel to be less difficult than he thought it would be.

Jacy missed Nitika and found comfort in talking to Reese. Once when he came by, Elizabeth was there and Reese introduced him. "Beth, this is my friend I've been telling you about."

"Well, now he'll be my friend, too," said Elizabeth, allowing a broad grin to explode across Jacy's face. Jacy warmed to her immediately. Unlike people who weren't Indians, she was curious about the boy and always liked talking to him whenever they met. She was especially interested in his time with Nitika, a favorite subject for Jacy, and he took delight in entertaining with little stories about the animal's antics.

Several times Reese asked Elizabeth to help him with research. She was always eager to do so and Reese was pleased to find her passionately interested in the material they gathered. They would often meet at the public library in Missoula, the most convenient place to work because it was located equidistant from Stevensville and Elk Woods. Early one morning Reese called Elizabeth. "What do you say to taking a break? Let's not work today. What do you usually do for fun?"

"The library is fun for me," Elizabeth said.

"You're always willing to work, but we've got to get away from the tedium. It looks like it's going to be a nice day; let's do something else."

Elizabeth thought for a moment. "Would you like to go fishing?"

"I can't believe you said that. Ever since I've been in Montana I've always wanted to go trout fishing. I wouldn't have thought to ask you to go."

"Why not?"

"It's a guy thing."

"Not for a Montana girl."

"Is that right?"

"Sure is. I'll bet I can outfish you."

"No way!"

"Yes way."

"I don't know about that. I've done my share."

"Me too. My father took me fishing when I was a little girl. My brother wasn't into it, so he took me. I love it."

Reese said. "Maybe Dalton English isn't so bad after all."

"He has his moments," Elizabeth laughed. "I haven't gone in a while, but living in Montana it's never far from my mind."

"Do you know where to go?"

"The Clark Fork and the Bitterroot rivers aren't too far, but we might be better off going up to Placid Lake. That's close and probably easier for a novice."

"Novice? You're referring to you, right?"

"No. You," she said.

"Me? You think I'm a novice?"

"I surely don't think I am."

"So you think you can outfish me."

"Why, of course. I'm a Montana girl, remember?"

Reese chuckled. "Novice, huh? We'll see about that."

"Jeff, my father is down in Wyoming. He went to a horse auction and will be gone a few days, so why don't you come here to pick me up?"

"All I need are directions."

"And a fishing license. I've already got mine," she said.

"Great. I love prepared competition. I'll pick one up on my way out."

Reese found Elk Woods easily and when he arrived, Elizabeth welcomed him in. Although he was impressed with the huge homestead, he felt uncomfortable as he looked around Dalton's enormous trophy room at the elk, mule deer and bear head mounts peering down with lifeless eyes from the eighteen-foot-high, teak paneled walls. "Does your father know about the work we're doing together?"

"J D seems to find out about everything," Elizabeth said with a shrug. "But I'm positive he doesn't know about your book or my helping you."

"Do you always call him J D?"

Elizabeth flinched, not realizing she used the initials. "No. Not always. But he doesn't mind. We kind of nettle each other with nicknames. I know it's nice that a girl calls her father daddy, but he hasn't always been a daddy."

She glanced at Reese. When she saw no reaction, she explained: "I use J D mostly when I want him to know I'm not pleased with him. He does the same thing with me. He calls me Lizzy. I don't like it, but if he knew that I was working on something that might put wolves in a better light, he'd be calling me a lot worse than that."

"I guess he'd be rough on you about that if he knew."

"He'd be furious. He knows of you and he probably knows I see you, but as for my being involved with anything positive about wolves, he'd go nuts on me."

"Then I guess it's best that he doesn't find out. The fish are waiting. Shall we go?"

They drove to the lake and spent most of the time laughing about which one was the better angler. They had more fun teasing one another than they did fishing, but still managed to end the day by catching several ten-inch rainbow trout. On their walk from the lake to Reese's Jeep, Elizabeth suggested they go to Elk Woods. "And, since I caught more fish than you did, you have to clean them. That's the rule."

"So you caught one more trout than I did, and you get to make up a rule?"

"Yes. You clean. I cook."

"Well, if I had my own fly rod, I'd have caught more," Reese said trying to hide a grin.

"No excuses. You clean."

"Okay, okay," Reese said, "but what do you say about going to my cabin instead of the ranch?"

Elizabeth looked at him. "You don't like it very much at Elk Woods, do you?"

Reese hesitated as he fumbled with the equipment he was packing. "It's one of the most beautiful places I've seen, but…"

"But it's not a home," she said. "I understand. I'll be more relaxed at your place, too."

As Reese drove to his cabin, Elizabeth cuddled close to him. "I really had fun today, Jeff. Did you?"

"It's been great - only I have to clean fish when we get back," Reese said with an exaggerated pout.

Elizabeth laughed. "I warned you that I was a good fisherman, but that aside, this was one of the nicest days I've spent in a long time. Thank you."

Jeff put his arm around Elizabeth's shoulder and drew her closer. "It's been a great day for me, too, and I'm glad it's not over."

* * *

After dinner that evening, Reese and Elizabeth sat talking. "What happens when you finish your book?" she asked.

Reese knew what Elizabeth was asking, but he avoided the answer. "I'll have to find a publisher, and go from there. My boss can really help with that."

Elizabeth was not going to let Reese escape so easily. "Will you go back to Chicago?"

Reese looked at her. He had asked himself the same question hundreds of times, and although he knew he had to return to his job, he found the answer difficult. "Beth," he said slowly lowering his eyes to the napkin he had folded neatly on his knee, "I have to go back. You know I do. What I don't know is how long I'll stay there."

Elizabeth's eyes glistened as they searched Reese's somber face.

She reached across the small oval table and put her hands on his upturned palms that beckoned her touch, and she felt the warmth of his skin meld into the coolness of hers. “I love you, Jeff. Whatever you decide is what I want most for you.”

Reese blushed with Elizabeth’s words and his answer came slowly as he tightened his hold on her hands. “Beth, I will come back.”

Elizabeth’s eyes welled up. “Promise you’ll come back to me?”

Jeffrey Reese tried never to make a promise he couldn’t keep. He had made a vow to love Samantha forever as she clung to her last hours of life. He never intended to break that promise and he agonized that loving again would do so. He could not bring himself to tell Elizabeth what she wanted to hear.

“I need time, Beth,” he said relaxing his hands allowing hers to be free. “I’ll be back one day. You’ll see.”

Elizabeth looked deeply into the blue eyes she had grown to adore. “Let’s do something different,” she said hoping to change the serious mood more for her benefit than for his. “Do you want to play cards?”

Thankful for the suggestion, Reese asked if she knew how to play Gin Rummy.

“I don’t think I’m too good.”

“Worse than fishing?” he said.”

Elizabeth laughed, “I showed you how to fish, didn’t I.”

“Okay. C’mon, I’ll teach you,” he said as he got a deck of cards and arranged two chairs at the kitchen table.

They sat across from one another and Reese pretended to roll up his sleeves and winked. As he dealt out cards, he asked Elizabeth about what she wanted most for her future.

“I’ve thought about it. I don’t ever want to leave Montana. Winters are tough, but the beauty is too much to give up. I’d like to get away for a while, though. Travel.”

“Why not just go. What keeps you?” he said.

“My mother lives in Montreal. I considered going there to visit her. I even got a passport last year thinking I’d take a trip, but I changed my mind.”

“Why?”

Elizabeth rose from the table, walked to a window and gazed out.

"It's a long story. Has a lot to do with my father and mother. I'll tell you about it sometime."

"I'm willing to listen," Reese said watching her return to the table.

"Another time."

Reese looked up from his cards and stared into Elizabeth's eyes. He sensed that she was concealing a hurt and switched the conversation. "Are you ready for your lesson?"

There was a stagnant moment as she glanced into Reese's eyes, but her upbeat nature would not allow the evening to spoil. She picked up her cards and flicked her hair. "Yes, I'm ready for my lesson," a full smile returning to her face.

When he saw the happy look, Reese felt an impulse to make a promise. He wanted to tell Elizabeth that he'd take her on vacation somewhere. Thinking it might be an impossible promise to keep, he fought the urge.

Reese considered himself a better than average gin player and thought of letting Elizabeth win. But after losing his third game by an embarrassing trouncing, he had to put a stop to his suffering.

"I give up," he said bumping his forehead with his palm in feigned annoyance. "If I take one more beating, I'll lose all self respect. This morning I get beat at fishing and now this. Do you know I put myself through college playing that game? Now I'm getting trounced by someone who tells me she's not too good."

"Oh, I was just lucky," Elizabeth said.

"You're lucky all right. Lucky you won't be here later to see me eat that card deck," he said with a pretended frown. "You killed me!"

"My middle name is Atkins, my mother's maiden name, but I'm changing it to Assassin."

"Appropriate," Reese said exaggerating the frown. As he did, he watched wrinkles begin at the dimples near the corners of Elizabeth's mouth bow through her lips, wave up through her cheeks and transform her entire face into a glorious smile that she held for a moment before bursting into laughter.

At that moment, Elizabeth's vitality overwhelmed Reese and he could not restrain his desire to hug her. He rose from the table, extended his arms to her as she stood and reached for him in a lingering embrace.

Like almost everything else, there was nothing awkward about the first kiss, but Reese noticed that she was unpracticed. He didn't think she felt at ease with it, because she mentioned her inexperience, so he asked for another.

He made her relax, held the awesome face in both hands, pressed his fingertips gently inward at the corners of her mouth to open it slightly and put his lips on hers. It was the perfect end to the night.

* * *

Two weeks passed. Reese was putting together the final chapters of his novel while Elizabeth spent as much time as she could helping him with the work. Reese had become more deeply involved with the woman and he knew saying goodbye would be more difficult than he had imagined.

The evening before he left on his drive back to Chicago, Elizabeth helped him pack his Jeep. "I made you some sandwiches for the drive," she said.

Reese giggled. "Chicken, I hope."

She chuckled back. "What else would I make for you?"

"Perfect," he said reaching to hug her. "I'll be thinking about you all the way back."

"I'll be thinking about you, too."

"I'll call you when I get there," Reese told her. The next thing he said surprised him as much as it did Elizabeth. "I *promise* I'll be back as soon as I can."

CHAPTER 21

**"I do not believe it is the wolves who need saving.
I believe it is the wolves' country that's endangered."
- Rick Bass, *The Ninemile Wolves***

As he grew older, Yuma's presence in the pack was becoming a problem. Aggression between him and the other males was more frequent, and Bartok challenged any advances he made toward the females. Yuma missed Anoki, and he mourned her. Poachers killed one of his littermates while another died of starvation, the result of a broken jaw from the kick of a bull moose. One of the only comforts remaining within the pack was his relationship with Dakota.

There stirred within the young wolf an atavistic impulse that he could neither understand nor ignore. Sometimes it took rise in his loins and drove him to disobedience. It often stirred in his head preoccupying his thoughts. It was always beyond his control; it was innate and he could not escape its force. He loved his pack life, but yearned to lead it, and herein his greatest dilemma. He understood that Bartok was the alpha, and Yuma had no desire to chance his father for the lead.

Yuma was becoming a loner, leaving the pack for hours, hunting on his own. Shako had delivered another litter of pups, swelling the pack to thirteen wolves, and Yuma did not find as much delight in the pups as the rest of the pack did. Even his closeness to Dakota was beginning to wane, and he found himself wanting more and more to wander.

Finally, early one evening, Yuma left the pack for good, loping into the twilight towards a new life. He set out to quell that ancient urge bred into his kind over three hundred thousand years before. The golden wolf had no direction, no purpose, no time limitations, only an innate drive, and he went with it. He heard the calls of his pack just as he had before, but chose to ignore them and ran farther into the night.

* * *

A male cardinal tweeted from the topmost branch of a lone, blue spruce and a distant raven argued with a magpie over a road kill. A warbler sang to its mate, a loon cried out and the bugling of a bull elk joined a woodland symphony as the sounds of dawn chimed in the Bitterroots. The first rays of an orange sun streamed through the canopy of stalwart cedars and Nitika awakened and stretched in its warmth. Curious to explore, she loped off towards a different life.

More than two miles away, Yuma awoke to the elk's reveille. Normally, the bugling would have excited the wolf, but without the pack, he knew the sound heralded nothing more than a memory. Alone, a different life awaited him and he trotted out to greet it.

Nitika's first encounter was with a large sow porcupine. When she recognized the animal, she approached it with caution. The porcupine did not run when it saw her, but turned its back and bristled, its devastating quills rattling in challenge. Nitika circled the porky, sniffing the familiar source of past pain. The lesson she learned as a pup was valuable, and unlike dogs that have tried to attack porcupines more than once, she quickly trotted away.

Two more nights passed before Nitika began to experience loneliness and the first pangs of hunger. She tried to catch a snowshoe rabbit, but the hare ran Nitika in circles before it headed downhill into the river-bottoms where it left her exhausted and thirsty. Frustrated, she lay panting for several minutes. After the pulse-beat in her ears diminished, she thought she heard something and sat up to listen. A soft noise crinkled beyond the brush line, and Nitika recognized it as the sound of water churning. She weakly got to her feet and headed for the icy creek that bubbled and splashed a short distance away.

* * *

Yuma had better luck. An excellent mouser, the wolf had no problem sating his appetite with voles and field mice before heading for water. Although far from his old territory, he knew how to locate a stream and headed towards the bottommost terrain he could find. As he got closer he could smell the creek, but he did not rush to it. Yuma knew that water was a magnet not only for prey, but for predators as well, and he knew better than to rush blindly into an area that might harbor an enemy. The wolf circled to approach the rill from downwind and his keen sense of smell made him hesitate as his nostrils filled with the odor of another canid. He stole towards the scent.

Nitika, standing chest high in the frigid brook, was gazing down into the gin-clear water when Yuma saw her. Brightly speckled brook trout darted to and fro nearly brushing against her knees. Preoccupied with the small, dark forms swimming close by her legs, she did not notice the wolf. Yuma watched as she made a wild stab with her muzzle only to spear a mouthful of water.

Nitika was so enrapt with trying to catch her dinner that she did not see Yuma sneak closer. She allowed the water to settle before making another lunge, but again came up without a fish. Lifting her head to shake water from her fur, she jerked back, startled to see Yuma only yards away.

Both animals stiffened to a trance, staring at each other for several seconds. Nitika was the first to move. She slowly emerged from the water, stopped and shook vigorously to expel the water from her coat into a myriad of microscopic droplets. A halo of mist from her fur caught the sunlight like a prism radiating a rainbow of colors into the surrounding air. Holding his head as high as possible, Yuma stood stately and unflinching as Nitika moved closer, bowing her head. Inches away from the regal wolf, she stopped.

Yuma's mane rippled as he slid around Nitika to approach her from behind, but she turned to face him with her own hackles raised. The wolf's keen nose had already informed him of her gender, but he did not relax his erect posture. There was something odd in this stranger that Yuma did not recognize, and he backed away.

The half dog in Nitika wanted to be friendly. The total wolf in

Yuma was much more guarded, and he turned to trot off. Nitika followed.

For the remainder of the day, Yuma tried to distance himself from Nitika. Her muscles ached to keep up with an animal that had greater strength and more stamina. But for her superior heart, she kept pace. By nightfall, the two had traveled many miles into the Idaho hills before Yuma decided to rest. Completely exhausted and ravenously hungry, Nitika was pleased the yellow wolf did not trek any farther and finally settled down. She curled up close enough to Yuma for her comfort, far enough away for his, and fell into an anxious sleep.

At times through the eons neither wraith nor spirit will steer the path of mortals; only chance will navigate the course. As it was for the fortunes of Nitika and Yuma, serendipity took the helm. Inexplicably, sometime during the night, nature's part in the grand scheme of fate played her role. Within the depths of Nitika's maturing body, her first ova released and her initial estrous cycle began.

When morning came, Yuma rose with a stretch and yawned. He looked over his shoulder and was not pleased to see that his follower was still nearby. The wolf moved away from his bed to relieve himself. Nitika, already awakened by an empty stomach, had begun to dig into a decomposing log. The sleep relieved Nitika's exhaustion, but her hunger went unabated. She had caught the scent of beetle larvae from beneath the rotting tree bark and pawed with wild determination to get at the source of the sweet smell.

Yuma watched the frantic activity for a moment, but his attention quickly turned to another matter. He had chosen the same spot in which to urinate that Nitika had used earlier, and he became alerted to a new condition of circumstance. The wolf, drawn by an allure that he was just beginning to understand, approached Nitika.

Some comprehension of his recent behavior began to manifest itself. It was part of the reason he had distanced himself from his pack mates, had been at odds with Bartok, and felt the need to leave his pack. As Yuma got closer to Nitika, he posed in the alert carriage of an alpha male attentive to a female.

Nitika stopped foraging in the soft wood and stiffened when she realized that Yuma was slinking toward her. The wolf, stirred by newly-found interest, circled the smaller female. Nitika, unlike the first time Yuma approached her, stood still.

CHAPTER 22

"We perceive the wolf to be the mythologized epitome of a savage ruthless killer which is, in reality, no more than a reflex image of ourselves."

- Farley Mowat, *Never Cry Wolf*

In the following days the golden wolf felt an urgent sense of responsibility toward Nitika, and Nitika allowed dependency upon Yuma. The wolf paid Nitika nearly all of his attention. Except to pursue the many species of small animals he was now resigned to hunt, Yuma would not let the female out of his sight.

Summertime survival was easy. Nitika watched Yuma catch fish, voles, mice and other rodents. With the exception of Yuma's ability to snag an occasional bird, Nitika got the idea and before the heat of the season ended, she, too, was able to hunt efficiently. But winter would hazard with a more difficult set of problems.

With the snows, Yuma knew the time of hibernation would come. Beavers, ground squirrels and many other animals would no longer be easy prey. Autumn would soon come to a close, and the wolf became restless. Although Nitika never thought about the rigors that winter would bring, Yuma did, and he led the way out of the bottoms. Both animals loped toward a difficult way of life.

Yuma was instinctively concerned about his mate's chances of bearing young successfully without the help of a pack. Although Yuma was an accomplished hunter, he needed the pack to provide

Nitika with the necessary nourishment to sustain her and her expected offspring. He knew that he might not be able to bring down healthy prey by himself. But he was not aware the following months could prove to be the worst that winter would offer.

For several days Yuma searched the higher elevations. Nitika was uncertain about the wolf's insistence to leave the river bottom. She did not know the larger animals wolves hunted in winter were the motivations behind Yuma's move, but her motivations were different; the stirring of life in her womb urged her to search for shelter.

The first storm of the season swept through north-central Idaho on wind gusts that slung icy rain against Yuma's muzzle. The sleet stung at the wolf's nose like a swarm of hornets with glass wings and he forged forward into the gale, shielding Nitika with his body. The pregnant female followed so close to Yuma that she was able to bury her face into the thick fur of his flanks whenever he stopped to gather his bearings.

As evening gray shrouded the last glimmer of daylight, Yuma was able to lead Nitika to the base of a shale wall outcrop. A slab of the flat stone protruded outward horizontally for several feet, forming a shelf-like overhang. Yuma circled beneath it several times tamping the freshly-fallen snow before he lay down and curled up. Nitika, for protection from the wind, cuddled to his side and both mates fell asleep with surprising ease.

* * *

As Nitika stirred to awaken, she felt a blanket of warmth about her. During the night snow covered her completely. It was the first time that she had ever slept out in a winter storm, and the unexpected comfort pleased her.

Yuma, already awake, squinted into the white of the snowy hills far in the distance. Nitika bounded to his side and nipped playfully at his muzzle, and he enthusiastically played back, bowling her over into a drift. The animals were forming a bond between them, and their affection for one another was growing steadily. Both canids were feeling a devotion that would endure for their lifetimes. They frolicked for several moments before Yuma trotted away and Nitika dutifully followed.

Two miles into the foothills, Yuma slowed his pace and then stopped. The wolf's ears slanted back and downward, the fur on his neck stiffened and a low growl rumbled in his throat. Nitika sidled to him and quickly caught the scent to which he reacted.

Thirty yards in front of Yuma, a wisp of steam filtered lazily upward through the snow from the base of a tremendous tamarack stump, a telltale sign of a denned animal. Nitika did not recognize the smell of the lynx in its lair, but Yuma did and he growled louder so the cat would hear as he moved closer.

In an explosion of snow, the lynx burst from its den when it heard Yuma's growl. The big tom arched its back and snarled as it took a menacing stance in front of Yuma, prepared to defend itself. Nitika, fearless as always, skulked towards the lynx, her intent more for curiosity than harm. The cat grew furious, brandishing razor-like claws and needle-sharp teeth, warning Nitika as it hissed and spit at the approaching enemy. Yuma had no intention to fight the animal, but as it lunged at Nitika, he attacked. A lightning fast swipe of the cat's paw slashed Nitika's left ear, but before the lynx could recoil, Yuma's jaw clamped on the cat's shoulder, sinking dagger-like fangs up to their hilt.

The thirty-five pound lynx was beyond the size of an average male, but even with its total fury unleashed, the large tom was tossed like a kitten in the jaws of a beast. Yuma outweighed the cat by over a hundred pounds and it was evident as he shook the animal lifeless.

Had Nitika held back, the lynx would not have been killed. Yuma's only interest was to flush the animal from its lair to secure a den for his mate. But when he saw the lynx strike at Nitika, his protective instinct fixed the cat's doom.

Nitika had her first brush with the dangers that lay ahead for her and her unborn pups. She watched as Yuma towed the repugnant lynx away from its den site and covered it with muddy snow and debris. Yuma returned to inspect the spacious cavity the cat had excavated under the hollow tamarack stump. Nitika saw what would now be her den, only a small advantage against the impossible odds she and Yuma would face in the following months.

CHAPTER 23

"We are drawn to wolves because no other animal is so like us. Of all the rest of creation, wolves reflect our images back to us most dramatically, most realistically, and most intensely."
- Peter Steinhart, *The Company of Wolves*

The snows deepened and the temperatures dropped to eight below zero. November had not yet arrived, but a fierce Idaho winter had. Yuma was having trouble. He had more than he could deal with fighting the deep snow. He missed his pack. They would take turns bulldozing paths through heavily drifting snow, but alone, he found following an elk herd impossible. He became exhausted on any excursion that took him far from the den, and hunger weakened his efforts to travel even a short distance to hunt.

Scavenging for the remains of winterkill was often futile. Other predators would beat him to such finds, and without the aide of other wolves, he could not seize the meat from most of his adversaries. Nitika, weakened by her condition, could not help, and both began to suffer the throes of starvation.

Because a feline is a repulsive enemy, Yuma preferred not to eat the meat of a cat, but survival made its demands. On one occasion he became so desperate that he dug for the lynx carcass he had buried weeks before. Yuma discovered that skunks had beaten him to it, their noisome musk fouling what little remained of skin and bones. Once again, Yuma returned to the waiting Nitika without sustenance for his starving mate, but he would not give up despite his depleted energy.

He would cast out again, day after day, foraging for anything he could bring to Nitika. Finally, Yuma came upon some luck. He heard the argument of ravens and left Nitika's side to investigate. The birds, circling in the sky not more than a mile from the den site, had found the whole carcass of a mule deer buck. The deer had succumbed to the rigors of the rut and the severity of a harsh winter. Yuma got to it before any other scavengers.

With only birds to protest, Yuma attempted to drag the deer to Nitika. In his weakened condition, the wolf fought the snow, pulling the carcass foot by foot, inch by grueling inch. For over an hour the exhausted and thoroughly drained wolf worked with every fiber of remaining strength to get the deer back to the den. The buck was big and its antlers got entangled in underbrush as Yuma's feet slipped on the icy terrain. Losing his grip on nearly every uphill tug, Yuma's effort was doubled further exhausting him as the deer slid backwards. After each yard of progress, he needed to stop for rest. He had only traveled half the distance when he used his final surge of energy, and then collapsed beside the deer.

Yuma fell into a fitful sleep, intermittently awakened by the quarrelsome ravens and the constant fear that he might lose his prize to other scavengers. After an hour, Yuma stood up on wobbly legs and tugged at the carcass, but could only move it a short distance. Then, his worst fears were realized.

A band of coyotes, alerted by the ravens, came upon the scene. When Yuma saw them, rage bristled through the ruff of the back of his neck; he knew instantly that he might lose all that he had worked for. Adrenalin flushed into his veins and Yuma was able to drag the deer another hundred yards before losing his grip and falling backwards. Sensing his vulnerability, four coyotes drew closer to the wolf than they would ever have dared.

Yuma got to his feet and snarled at the coyotes, causing them to separate and dance in and out, grabbing at the meat from different directions. Yuma was becoming desperate, and the thought of failure consumed what little spirit remained in his gut as he glanced around to check for an escape route. With a quick look to his left, Yuma noticed a lodgepole pine stump a few yards away. It was a stump with a history about which Yuma knew nothing. All he knew was that if he could get his back to it, he would be able to face the threatening foursome more easily and protect his precious find. This he knew from experience, not from logic. Logic was not in Yuma's mental makeup, but memory was.

Whenever he and his pack surrounded an animal and attacked it in the open, the prey was at a disadvantage. If a side was shielded from attack, victims were less vulnerable, and Yuma wanted that advantage. But the wolf could hardly stand, let alone drag his bounty to the stump.

It was not with uncanny reasoning, but with good luck that Yuma's subsequent actions were successful. The wolf knew the coyotes only wanted the deer and not him, but he also knew that giving up the deer could mean doom for him and his mate.

He circled the carcass and got into a position with the dead deer and the stump in front of him and then slowly backed up. Begrudgingly, he was conceding the prize in exchange for his life. When the coyotes saw Yuma retreat, they rushed for the carcass, pulling it away from the wolf -- and toward the stump.

Yuma glared with vengeful eyes as the coyotes attempted to get the carcass as far from him as they could. When Yuma saw the foursome drag the deer close to the stump, he feigned a charge, snarling and snapping. For an instant, the four coyotes reacted and bolted a short distance from the deer, but their retreat was enough. It allowed Yuma the fortune he needed, and with a few bounds he was able to get between the deer carcass and the stump.

Yuma lay panting, his back to the huge stump, and his front paws nearly touching the mule deer. Several yards beyond, the coyotes yelped in annoyance. Their advantage of harassing the wolf from behind was lost and they paced to and fro in frustration before deciding to abandon the effort entirely.

Cowards at heart, with little confidence to test the mettle of any wolf's character, the coyotes loped off and Yuma relaxed. Had they realized the wolf could not muster the energy to fight them, the four bandits could easily have stolen the carcass, but Yuma was fortunate for their timidity.

After a long rest, Yuma resumed the onerous chore. Struggling mightily, with no reserve of energy remaining in his shaking body, sheer willpower awarded the yellow wolf his goal. Just before nightfall he managed to lug the life-giving prize to the portal of the den.

Nitika crawled from the mouth of the lair and wriggled to her belly greeting him with whimpers and squeals of delight. She paid more attention to her exhausted mate than she did to the deer, and hours passed before either she or Yuma was able to feed. The golden wolf had succeeded in saving his mate, but the four pups that Nitika carried in her womb were lost, absorbed by her body and weeks of starvation.

The rest of winter would hold other hardships for Nitika and Yuma, but none so severe that Yuma could not negotiate. The flesh of the large, mule deer buck sufficed for weeks, and with Nitika's regained strength, the healthy pair was able to forage adequately for a meager existence for the remainder of winter.

Yuma had led a lifestyle of cooperation before dispersing from his pack. Dependent upon his own kind to survive, life within the pack was as much a part of Yuma's nature as his desire to strike out on his own and reproduce. The wolf needed his pack.

As the remainder of the winter months passed, Yuma's resolve and Nitika's resiliency led to much of their success. Nitika adapted and learned to hunt, but luck, also, played her part. Yuma knew that life in the pack was less subject to chance, and he instinctively yearned to return to an existence of collaboration. When the long, cold season finally came to a close, the golden wolf led his mate on a search for a different life.

CHAPTER 24

**"They're a lot like us, a social creature bonded by family."
- Nick Jans, Alaskan author/photographer**

Nitika watched as Yuma climbed atop the trunk of a black cottonwood deadfall, threw back his head and bellowed into the dusk. The howl pierced the silence of a slumbering forest and beckoned through the age-old ponderosa pines. The nocturnal fauna paid attention. A raccoon stood on its hind legs to listen; martins, hares and weasels scurried for cover. A band of coyotes cowered together, a porcupine stopped its waddle to silence the rattle of quills so it could hear, and a screech owl took flight on silent wings to race the sound.

Yuma listened for a response, but when he heard none, he set out on a purposeful journey. Several times during the night Yuma called whenever he stopped to rest. Finally, one of his bellows cleared the top of the tree line, spilled out over the Bitterroot valley and onto a granite bench to the ears of a distant wolf pack.

Dakota and Bartok rose to their feet and cocked their heads. Shako was the first to respond as the alpha female recognized the voice of her son. Bartok was the only wolf to join her in answering. When he heard the bay of his father, a shiver raised Yuma's hackles and he loped off into what remained of the night and traveled doggedly towards his old den site with Nitika in tow.

Dawn blushed the winter landscape into a blue-orange hue as it filtered through the boughs of a great Douglas fir. Dakota, ever the lookout, was the first to spot Yuma and Nitika trudging over a distant rise through the purple tinted snow. Dakota's yelp to Bartok had the alpha male and Shako bounding toward their son.

The display among the reuniting wolves was a show of sheer jubilation, and Yuma whirled and tumbled to its joy, squealing and lapping affection upon every wolf he recognized. Even the pups gamboled into the delight, hopping and yipping to get Yuma's attention. Nitika stood silent and still, watching the spectacle. Only the tip of her tail was uncontrollable as it wagged tentatively from side to side.

Slowly, the pack turned to Nitika as Bartok circled the stranger, sniffing and probing curiously at the rigid female. Following his lead, the pack satisfied its curiosity about Nitika. Every wolf sensed the strangeness in her. Those more skeptical among the pack were more tentative, but they all knew that she had been in Yuma's company and that afforded her a fortuitous advantage. Their keen senses told every wolf many things about Nitika, but the most obvious was that in her womb stirred three new lives, the greatest joy of any pack. When the group realized her condition, the focus of attention, even by Bartok and Shako, was immediate and her acceptance complete.

CHAPTER 25

"I know this much. They are much misunderstood, but they are smart, cunning, and important to the overall balance of our threatened ecosystem. They are more than worth preserving."
- Robert Redford

John Dalton English took immense pride in his ten thousand acre ranch in the foothills of the Bitterroot Mountains. The pastoral beauty of the property was as envied as Dalton's enormous wealth. An occasional whitetail deer, small herds of Roosevelt elk and thousands of Black Angus cattle often grazed right up to the portals of his sprawling home.

Lights from the lower floors of the big house began to flick on as evening shadows lengthened to cloak the landscape of Elk Woods. Inside, Dalton sat behind an oversized mesquite-wood desk raking his fingers through thick, scruffy brown hair that defied the comb and belied his age. For most of his seventy years, the man's slender stature was erect and he walked with the swagger of a drill sergeant, but the years bent his posture, making it necessary for him to slightly tilt his head back in order to make eye contact with his visitor.

Dalton propped his strong lower jaw on his thumb and index finger. His eyes, though tired, held a stare of intent like those of a hunting cat focusing upon its prey. The brown eyes revealed a past of pain, yet they denied the truth with a compensating defiance as though prepared for a challenge. Slouched before him in a tufted brown leather chair was Martin Kerns, a heavy-set man dressed in khaki fatigues and paratrooper boots.

Kerns gawked at the ceiling-high bookshelf that took up an entire wall of the room. "You read all these books J D?"

Dalton had read even more books than were in his collection, but he knew that Kerns wouldn't appreciate the truth so he just shook his head in disgust. "Books are not your thing, are they Muzzy?"

Kerns grinned. "Who needs all them books," he said as he held out an empty Coors can and shook it playfully at Dalton before answering his own question. "Not me."

Dalton ignored Kern's hint for another beer and continued to shake his head. "No, I wouldn't think so."

Kerns' grin grew even broader. "You still worried about ole Charlie?"

Dalton kept glaring at Kerns. "Worried? Yeah, I'm worried. I'm afraid you might screw this whole thing up."

Kerns' voice got bear-like and demanding. "J D, I ain't afraid of Whittington. Don't you worry none. He ain't seen 'em, so he don't know nuthin' about 'em. I'm the only one who knows they're livin' up there. Besides, I got more to worry about than you. Now, whattaya say about another beer?"

Dalton again ignored the man's request as he shifted from behind his desk and staggered to rise. Leaning shakily forward to support himself on his knuckles, Dalton raised his voice. "Whittington knows I'll kill every last wolf around. He'll think I set out the poison."

"I tell ya, Whittington ain't gonna know nothing. Just as long as you don't buy no strychnine, they can't prove you was involved."

Dalton pointed a finger at Kerns. "You better not mess this up, Muzzy. I'm serious."

"You worry too much. Lemme handle it. Now, how about that beer?"

"No. No more beer. I want you sober so you can take care of this thing."

"No two beers gonna get me drunk, J D."

"I said no!"

"For cryin' out loud, no more beer? And ya don't even let a guy smoke around here," Kearns groaned. "Okay. Then how about my money?"

Dalton tottered from behind his desk and ambled toward the door nodding his head. "When I see the dead wolves; you'll see the money."

Kerns wasn't happy and he mumbled under his breath as he was being led from the room. Dalton paused when he saw Kerns toss the empty beer can towards the bookshelf. "If you want to work for me, Muzzy, you'd better pick that up."

Kerns headed for the beer can. "I ain't seen nobody like you, J D. I'm the only guy who can do what you want and you won't gimme the time of day."

"You're right. You're the only person I know who enjoys killing. You'd do it without pay. And, you're right about another thing. I wouldn't give you the correct time if I had Big Ben strapped to my back. Now let's go."

Elizabeth heard it all. She stood glaring at her father as he emerged from the library to escort his guest out. Behind Dalton's back, Kerns hesitated, turned his head to ogle Elizabeth and smirked. His eyes bore into the girl, stripping her naked as he spoke to Dalton: "J D, I'll call when it's done. I'll get it done, don't worry about nuthin."

The man shuffled to the door, turned to give Elizabeth a parting glance and waddled down the long stone walk to his truck. Dalton craned his neck turning to Elizabeth and snapped at her. "Lizzy, eavesdropping again?"

"Don't call me that, dad. You know I don't like it."

Turning his back to his daughter, Dalton wobbled down the vaulted hallway lined with marble statues of Roman emperors. On the walls behind the statues, huge oil paintings of hunting scenes adorned the long corridor. As he made his way to the bar, he turned to see that Elizabeth was following him.

"I don't like you snooping into my business," he said as he poured several fingers of Johnny Walker Black into a water glass, lifted it to his nose and sniffed as though the booze had an aroma to surpass the bouquet of the most fragrant flower.

Dalton swirled the liquor and continued to smell the glass as Elizabeth watched. "I'm not snooping, J D. I know what you're planning. Why do you deal with that awful man?"

"Muzzy?"

"Yes. Kerns. He's horribly rude."

Dalton took a mouthful of scotch and gulped it down. "So, he's got bad manners. I don't give a flying fiddle about that."

"Do you care that he leers at me behind your back? He gives me the chills."

"He serves a purpose. I told you. I don't care about his manners."

"What purpose, J D? Killing wolves?"

"Get off that kick. You know my take on it and I'm not about to let some sniveling skirt interfere with how I run my business. You're like your mother."

Elizabeth looked into her father's raging eyes and spoke softly. "What will you do J D, force me to run out of here like you did her?"

"Damn it!" Dalton screamed. "That cheating bitch wasn't forced. Ran on her own. Abandonment! That's what the documents say. You should know that by now."

Elizabeth knew more about it than she was willing to admit. She knew her mother's leaving was her own decision. She knew about the other man and that her mother turned her back on Dalton months before his temperament began to change and his drinking became an issue.

But she wasn't about to forgive his bitterness. "So take it out on the wolves," she said as she watched Dalton caress the glass of scotch before taking another gulp.

"This spread pays the bills. Wolves and people who defend them don't!"

"Wolves don't hurt your business. And you know it. How many heifers have you lost to them?"

Dalton took another big swig of his drink, nearly emptying the glass. He tried to control himself, lowering his voice. "None. That's because I'll kill every one of those vermin I can. If other ranchmen did the same, we'd have no problem."

"No! That's not the answer. If they can possibly help it, wolves would prefer to hunt in the wild rather than come anywhere near where people are."

"Where do you get your information? You talk like ranch owners have never lost livestock to wolves."

"The ranchers are compensated for any animals wolves take. How many times has that been necessary? Bears and cougars kill more calves than wolves ever do."

"If every tree hugger has a say, it'll be too late. I can't believe my own daughter can't see that. I know where you get your BS from, Lizzy. Don't for a minute think I don't."

Elizabeth gave her father a quizzical look. "Who are you talking about?"

"That writer, wolf lover you were hanging around with when he was here causing trouble. He's gotten into your head."

"Jeff Reese?"

"Bet you thought I didn't know about your little affair," he said finishing what remained in his glass.

"I didn't try to hide our relationship from anyone."

"I can't believe you were stuck on a slicker. A wolf kisser, no less."

Elizabeth ignored his remark. "Daddy, I just think there's a better way than hiring someone like Muzzy Kerns to kill wolves."

"Kerns knows stuff I need to know. He works for the conservation department and gets information I don't have."

Elizabeth looked away. "That's terrible."

"Terrible? I'll tell you what's terrible. Kerns knows of a wolf den not far from here. Says a whole pack lives there. One of the biggest he's ever seen in these parts."

"Have they bothered anyone? Have they troubled you?"

"I tell you it's going to be a problem unless we do something."

"No. Leave them alone. Please!"

"No, Lizzy. You leave me alone. Where did you learn your disrespect? You have more respect for the goddamned wolves than you do for me."

"No, J D. I don't disrespect you, I just don't respect some of the things you do."

"Like I told your brother, if you don't like the way I operate, don't let the door clip your skinny backside as you walk out."

Elizabeth watched her father refill his glass to the rim, his shaky hand unable to keep the liquid from overflowing. She was aware of how nasty he would become when he drank. "Daddy, don't. Don't drink more."

"Don't drink! Don't do this! Don't do that! That sure sounds like an Atkins to me. Aside from nagging me about the freaking wolves,

Lizzy, you sound like you mother."

"Why can't you realize that you need people? Don't you see how difficult it is to care about you? Sometimes you make it hard for people to love you when you say things like that."

"Your mother didn't love anything about me. All she cared about was straying around like some alley cat. She couldn't stand it when I got sick."

"She couldn't stand what made you sick. The drinking made her leave."

Dalton peered into his daughter's eyes. "Maybe her straying make me drink?"

Elizabeth returned her father's stare. She knew he had a point. "I'm sorry, daddy. It's been a long time since then."

"Yes, it has, and the door didn't bump her butt as she went, either. She flew out of here like a bat outta hell, and I'm better for it."

"Is that what you want? First it was Jamie, then it was mom. Do you want to drive me from your life, too?"

Dalton gave an exaggerated shrug and toasted his glass toward his daughter. Elizabeth closed her eyes so she wouldn't see him guzzling his glass dry, turned slowly away from the familiar scene and quickened her step as she climbed the broad, Titanic-like staircase to her second-story bedroom.

When Elizabeth opened the door, the unlighted room felt larger than it was, too vast to contain the warmth of closeness she wanted to feel. She needed the usual comfort her bedroom provided whenever she'd retreat there to escape her father's moody tantrums. Her bedroom, ever the sanctuary, was not merely where she slept, but where she'd go to reminisce about the better days at Elk Woods. It was where she'd go to think about her future, where she'd fantasize about meeting the man of her dreams.

Now, the room had become the place where she'd go to think about Jeff Reese, where she'd write letters to him, where she'd telephone him to hear the comfort of his voice, and where she hoped to hear the words he'd say to bring her greatest joy. The room was always a place where life seemed cheerful and bright, but as she entered now, its purpose might offer only sleep, no consolation to escape her gloom.

Despair had taken over Elizabeth's spirit and she was afraid the room's darkness would only intensify her doldrums: the feeling of being swallowed into an abysmal, black throat. The bottomless gullet that would devour her mind had to be avoided. She knew sleep would not be possible, so one by one she turned on the lights.

A double-tiered brass, chandelier sent an array of colors from its prism crystals sparkling across the cathedral ceiling, and Elizabeth's disposition lightened. She tugged the pull-chain of a multi-colored Tiffany lamp; its glow through the intricate glasswork, further brightened her mood. Elizabeth walked to her bedside and switched on a table light she used for reading. There, at its base, she picked up a copy of Reese's manuscript. As she leafed through it, a feeling of warmth melted away the last of her sadness and she picked up the phone to dial Reese.

Reese sat alone in his Chicago efficiency flat reading *Defenders of Wildlife* magazine. In disbelief, he reread the lines aloud: "The Alaska Board of Game has targeted 900 wolves to be killed through approved aerial hunts. Coupled with legal hunting and trapping, one-third of Alaska's wolf population will be destroyed."

A gale of depression blew through him as though his efforts to calm the winds of negativity about the wolf were as helplessness as a leaf in a tornado, and he flung the magazine aside. He rose to his feet to pace and talk to himself. "Can this be happening again? I can't believe people still don't get it. Just leave the damned things alone, for God's sake."

Reese searched the walls of his apartment and felt them move closer and closer squeezing him into a feeling of hopelessness. He walked to a window, looked outside at the evening traffic and found himself wishing he were back in his Montana cabin.

He thought about Elizabeth and began to realize how much he missed her. He thought about how much fun it was to spend time with her. He wanted to hear her laughter; he wanted to feel her touch and to be comforted by her. He realized how empty his life was without her, and as he reached for the phone, its ring startled him. The possibility that he was about to be sidetracked from calling her rushed fear into his chest and he let the phone ring until the answering machine picked up.

"Hello, Jeffrey. It's me. I was just thinking about you and I wanted to talk, but I guess…."

A fresh gust of Rocky Mountain air swept through the room. Elizabeth's voice foisted his spirits and Reese grabbed the receiver. "Beth. I'm here!"

"Hi Jeff. Are you busy?"

"No, no. I was just… I was just thinking about you. I was just about to call you."

The scars of past memories had all but dissolved.

CHAPTER 26

"Hardly a man of the thousands to come on hundreds of planes and ships, but wanted to kill a wolf."
- Lois Crisler, *Arctic Wild*

Several days passed since Martin Kerns spoke to Dalton at Elk Woods, and since Elizabeth had telephoned Reese. Carrying enough strychnine to poison every wolf in Montana, Kerns drove his ATV for two hours into a densely wooded area of the Bitterroot Mountains. The four-wheeler groaned and clunked over the rugged terrain straining to bear the three-hundred-pound weight of its passenger and his insidious cargo.

Kerns thought about the countless wolves he had slain in the past and grinned. "I'll make a fortune on these new bastards," he said to himself. "So long as they don't die where I can't find 'em."

Kerns knew of the penalty he'd face for poaching wolves in the Bitterroots if Whittington ever found out. He knew he'd be jailed and fined, and he also realized his livelihood was at stake. If there was one thing Martin Kerns could not afford, it was to lose his job. No one in Stevensville, or for that matter, anywhere else he was known would ever employ him.

His vulgarity was not limited to his language, but soiled into his personal mannerisms as well. An unkempt man, Kerns poked and prodded at his bodily folds, skin crevasses and scruffy, oily goatee, but his ears and nose were favorite targets no matter his company.

When Charles Whittington was transferred from Canada to chief conservation officer in the Stevensville district, he inherited Kerns as a clerk. Whittington was simply too kindhearted to fire a man who had preceded him in the field office, and he tolerated Kerns despite his indecencies. Kerns was fortunate that Whittington was able to withstand criticism for keeping him on, but Kerns, lacking any redeeming qualities, did not appreciate the tolerance his boss possessed. Whittington was about to be repaid for his kindness. Martin Kerns headed into the mountains and continued to talk to himself.

"Old Whitty would crap himself if he knew I killed more wolves than anyone. That Chad McKittrick slob got caught when he shot that wolf from Yellowstone. But they ain't catchin' me. I ain't gonna get fined. Damned fools! They shoulda made a hero outta old Chad instead of takin' him to court and fining him like they did. Big deal. He shoots a wolf an has to pay a fine 'cause it had a collar on it. That's a laugh. At least these wolves around here don't have no collars."

As the clattering chug of a worn engine disturbed the serenity of a rustic landscape, a family of wolves more than six miles away heard the intrusion and became restless. The pack's leader listened as the din of man approached, and when he realized the noise was coming still closer, he chased three pups into a den-cave beneath a hemlock overhang. Then he turned and barked to his pack-mates.

All of the pack's adult wolves scurried to round up the juveniles and herd them into a nearby ravine away from the den site. Only a big alpha male and two other wolves stayed behind. Their intent was to protect their home and the puppies.

Kerns was amazed as he neared the area in which he knew the den to be. There, in the distance, he saw three wolves standing erect and intent atop a rise. They stared in his direction. Kerns stopped his vehicle and drew a Remington .22/250 out of a scabbard from the rear of his four-wheeler and shakily levered a bullet from the magazine into the chamber.

Confused as to why the wolves did not flee as they usually did, Kerns dropped to his belly and slithered along the ground to a better vantage point. His heart pounding, his foul breath huffing, he slinked to a small knoll and peeked over to see the wolves had not moved.

"What the hell are they doing?" he said to himself. "Why ain't they runnin' away?"

He steadied his rifle on a mound of sphagnum moss to look through the scope at the three wolves. For a moment he thought they may not have seen him, but as he squinted into the rifle's scope, he realized the stupidity of his thoughts. All three wolves stood side-by-side, still, tall and bold, their gazes fixed firmly on him.

Sweat pimpled on Kerns' forehead and oozed through thick, black brows into his rodent-like eyes as he tried to focus on the face of the largest wolf. Pausing to rake his sleeve across the bridge of his nose, he drew a deep breath and peered again through the telescopic sight. His pulse throbbed in his temples and the rifle jittered slightly as he fought to steady the weapon. Slowly, the image cleared in the scope and the man cringed. Kerns could see the rebellious fire of unblinking eyes burning into him like the defiant magma of an erupting volcano, and he was afraid.

Kerns' fear was not of attack by the three wolves glaring at him; it was of their conviction; it was fear of the wolf's resolve to survive. Despite the insurmountable odds of loyalty versus death, of fang versus gun, of wolf versus man, Martin Kerns was afraid of the relentless determination of the wolf's being.

Kerns saw in the eyes of a wolf, courage beyond anything he could muster; he saw emotion beyond any he could feel; and he saw an intelligent comprehension beyond that which he could understand. In an instant, the very nature of one of the Earth's most unique animals became apparent to a dense human being.

And he squeezed the trigger.

* * *

From a deep sleep, Jeff Reese jerked into a sitting position. His head ached violently and sweat seeped from his brow into widened eyes that searched the blurred darkness for the source of the explosions that had awakened him. As the earsplitting blasts of gunshots faded away, he held his breath listening. So real were the booming reports of a high-powered rifle that he dismissed the notion that another nightmare had startled him and he continued to listen. But Reese heard only silence as profound as deafness. Slowly, he began to realize the blasts that had reverberated in his aching head were merely echoes from his imagination.

In search of the time of day he staggered to his feet and dragged himself from the sofa where he had fallen asleep after Charles Whittington's phone call. He recalled the earlier conversation and the nauseating report. Whittington told him of three slain wolves near Stevensville, and the news so sickened Reese that he tried to shut it out of his mind.

The only way he knew to make pain go away never actually worked. He had failed before at other attempts to blot out disheartening news, and he was aware the drink would only make him groggy. Sometimes, the benumbed mind, like an anesthesia, led to sleep. Though sleep was of little consolation, the detested gin was worth the try.

He stared at a clock in disbelief to discover it was early evening. He had slept for only an hour, and through his grogginess, bits and pieces of reality emerged.

Reese remembered the drink. He had filled a glass with tomato juice to disguise the taste of Smirnoff. The report about the poached wolves was the reason he had taken the drink, and he knew the gin and the bad news were the catalysts for his dream that he now wanted to piece together.

Still in a daze, he felt the cold chisel of emptiness gouge at his stomach. He pulled a slice of leftover pizza from the refrigerator and started to boil water for instant coffee as he tried to make sense of his disturbed sleep. Images swirled in his mind. He flinched at the meaning of a dream about slain wolves, a grim killer and – an angelic messenger.

Again he looked at the clock, still trying to orient himself to the world around him. Everything was hazy white. It seemed as though he were trying to find his way through white fog. He sat on the arm of his sofa staring through the mist at the whistling, white porcelain teakettle, and slowly recalled the wolves.

Through the steam of the teapot, standing tall and ghostlike in front of their pack were three wolves, their pure white fur glistening in contrast to the colorless wolves cowering behind them. And beyond the wolves was the dark figure of a gunman taking aim, his searing red eyes glowed from a fiendish skull as though they belonged to the lord of Hell. Reese shuddered at the vision and no longer had any appetite for the pizza. He rose to turn off the burner. The spasms in his stomach, he decided, were not from hunger.

He filled a tall glass with ice and tap water, pressed it to his forehead before taking a swallow, and returned to the sofa to sit down. Keeping the cold glass to his forehead, he thought about the dream. He remembered hearing the whimper of pups and the mixture of barks and yelps from juvenile wolves, but the three white leaders did not vocalize as the others. They spoke in voices as human as Reese's.

"Stand, my brothers," he heard. "Fear not the two-legged beast. We must not run again."

"I will stand, my master," answered another. "I am with you and will not run."

The third wolf, smaller and whiter than the other two, stared directly at Reese with a look that peered into his mind. Reese could see in the eyes of the whitest wolf an intelligent gleam that seemed to understand the futility of its situation and it spoke to him. "Help us. Save us. We cannot stand alone."

Reese remembered trying to shout, urging them to run. He wanted to tell them to hide. He tried to scream out to them. But his tongue, he recalled, swelled and his lips thickened and words would not form. Only a plaintive yowl emerged before all fell silent and he was helpless to respond to the wolf's plea.

He saw himself turn to the gunman and try to run to him. His legs, bound in a mysterious twine, were unable to move. He was raking and pulling as he struggled to loosen the gluey cords from his thighs and knees, but he couldn't.

Few things disturbed Reese as much as Whittington's phone call and he squirmed as he realized he did not awaken to find relief from the nightmare. The conscious fact still remained. Three wolves were dead and he now was left with the images of their demise. But another image lay within the dream that would hold even more significance to Jeffrey Reese, and he strained to bring it back to light.

In the dream he remembered expecting the inevitable as he looked towards the wolves and watched in silent, slow-motioned horror. First, the largest wolf was hit and dropped to the ground in a lifeless shiver. The others lifted their heads to howl, but emitted no sounds. In silence the second wolf fell dead. Again there was no sound as the last wolf's defiant stance was met with quiet death. The absence of sound, Reese recalled, had him turn and glance at the wolf slayer.

Then, like an epiphany, Reese recalled the appearance of the bizarre scene; the killer had not yet fired his weapon. Something stopped him. Something had held him from shooting. Something or someone was standing in his way.

Struggling with recall, Reese fought to bring back the revelation of his dream. He rose from the couch for more water. He twirled the glass slowly watching the remaining ice melt into the swirling water and he remembered the incarnation. A woman had appeared.

Now, more recall came to him. He remembered that sound had returned to his dream and he could hear the faint whine of the wind as it swirled her hair like the liquid in his glass. In a gossamer gown, whiter than the glowing fur of the three wolves, a young woman stood in front of the poacher. Reese recalled watching as she raised her arms and held her palms inches from the muzzle of the shooter's rifle. She spoke to the gunman, her words barely audible. Though he could not see her face, Reese recognized the dulcet voice of Samantha.

As in all of his dreams of Samantha, there loomed a bittersweet joy. He would see her before him, beautiful, vibrant and alive, but in his subconscious mind, true mirth was always denied; and he would also see her pregnant, ill and dying.

Reese saw himself as he tried to walk and was surprised; his legs were no longer bound. He moved up behind her and was able to speak. "Sammy. Save them. Don't let him kill the wolves."

Reese even remembered Samantha's exact words: "No, Jeffrey. I came for you, not the wolves. There is no rescue for those souls," she cried, "but you can survive."

The voice was no longer that of a dying woman. He felt not the bittersweet aura of disappointment, but the exhilaration of true joy. His entire body lightened; the weight of his past disappeared with Samantha's words. As she turned to face him, he was looking into the eyes of Elizabeth English.

He remembered trying to reach out for her, but as in other dreams of Elizabeth he could not hold her. He called her name, but she did not answer. She looked into his eyes and slowly raised her hands up to shield her ears from the three deafening explosions that followed.

Booomm! ---------- Booomm! ---------- Booomm!

His heart pounded at the walls of his chest and he gulped in as much air as his begging lungs could hold. Then, Reese rose from the couch and searched the room to see if the white fog was gone. He listened for street sounds to make sure he could hear; he touched his face to ensure he could feel. Reese wanted to make certain he was awake.

He thought about the dream again and remembered Samantha's words. "Or were they Elizabeth's? Yes! It was Elizabeth," he said as he recognized the truth of his own consciousness. His life was going to be different.

Without the scars of past memories to mar the loveliness of his intentions, Jeff Reese reached for the telephone.

When she answered the phone, Elizabeth's voice never sounded as sweet. "Hi, Jeff. How are you?"

"I've never felt better in my entire life."

"That's great. I wasn't expecting you to call, but I'm glad you did."

"I've got something to tell you."

Elizabeth thought she noticed a serious tone. "What is it, Jeff?"

"I've been thinking about you. I've thought about coming back."

"Oh, my gosh! That's great! When?"

Reese didn't acknowledge her enthusiasm. He was thinking about how he should broach a delicate subject. He chose his words carefully. Pausing to collect his thoughts, Reese drew a deep breath.

"I got a call from Charley Whittington a few hours ago about some wolf killings up there and I'm going to ask my boss for some time to look into it."

"Oh, God, no!"

Elizabeth's shriek startled Reese. "Beth! What's the matter?"

"Oh, God! I think my father has done something horrible. Jeff, I think he may be responsible somehow," she said, her voice beginning to crack.

"What did he do?"

Elizabeth began to cry. "I overheard him talking about --- about killing wolves in our area."

Reese waited for her to catch her breath. "Did he say he was planning to do it, or has he already done it?"

"Both, I think. He's always talked about it. And I thought that's all it was. Just talk. But just recently I overheard him planning to do it. They planned to wipe out a whole wolf family," she sobbed.

"It wasn't a whole family," Reese said. "Whittington told me there were three wolves, so you may be wrong. Three, Beth, not a whole pack."

"No, please, please. I hope it's not true. My own father. I feel terrible. I…"

As Elizabeth cried into the phone, Reese tried to console her. "Beth. Listen to me. I need you to be strong right now. Okay?"

Reese waited until she regained her composure. "There's another reason I'm coming back."

He took another deep breath and let it out slowly. Reese never felt as unsure of himself as he did that moment. He gulped more air as he uttered the words he thought he'd never be able to say. "I'm coming to see you because -- I know that I love you."

Elizabeth swallowed to keep from sobbing again, struggling to get the words out. "I love you, Jeffrey Reese. I love you so much. You have no idea how I've wanted to hear you say that to me."

Overwhelming warmth filled him. It felt as though his heart had doubled, then tripled in size, getting larger and larger. It was as if his heart had grown big enough to envelop Elizabeth and everything about her. The sensation was one he had not felt in years and he wanted to freeze-frame it forever. His desire to take Elizabeth into his arms at that moment was so intense he could not contain his feelings. "I love you, Beth. I honestly love you, too. I'm coming to see you --- to ask you to marry me."

Elizabeth basked in Jeff's words. Her emotions welled up from her heart and swelled her throat; for a moment she was unable to speak.

The silence from the receiver lasted long enough for Reese's thoughts to race back to all of the conversations he had ever had with Elizabeth. Talk of marriage never came up. As far as he knew, it wasn't a part of Elizabeth's plans. Reese had just made a proposal and he didn't know whether Elizabeth had ever intended to get married.

Spiked by panic, adrenalin pumped into Reese's veins, his ears drummed with each of his heartbeats and he could hardly hear Elizabeth talking. He thought he heard her crying. He switched the phone from one hand to the other to listen more closely.

Elizabeth was crying and trying to talk at the same time. "Jeffrey. You don't know," she sobbed. "You have no idea how I prayed."

Catching her breath more steadily she began to calm. "I wished for you to say you loved me since I first met you. I thought about you constantly. Every day you were in my thoughts, on my mind, in my dreams. I prayed that you'd come for me one day and that you'd want to marry me."

For Elizabeth, the proposal opened her heart, and her love for Reese poured out in words and tears. She spoke and cried until her sobs slowly transformed into sounds of delight.

For Reese, his declaration was one he had wanted to make for a long time. Though the words came, others did not easily follow and he was glad that Elizabeth was able to regain her composure and conclude the moment with feel-good relief.

"And, by the way," she beamed. "Happy birthday!"

"That's right," he said with a laugh. "I forgot all about it. Tomorrow is my birthday."

"I know," she said. "Tomorrow is your birthday."

Reese and Elizabeth talked for more than an hour longer than they had ever talked before. They explored each other's wishes and dreams, neither wanting to break the conversation, neither wanting to lose the other's presence.

CHAPTER 27

"While wolves are often portrayed as villains, our experience told a different story. We witnessed many acts of compassion and kindness in the three wolf families we observed."

- Helen Thayer, *Three Among the Wolves*

When Reese pulled into *The National Graphic's* parking lot the next morning, he could not remember anything about his commute. To him there were no other drivers on the road. He could not recall a single traffic light, or any of the streets he had taken to get there. The call from Whittington, the dream, his call to Elizabeth and his talk with Jacy blanked his awareness of everything else.

As he stepped from his Jeep, he searched his pockets to quell the lingering notion that he had forgotten something. In his shirt pocket was a package pick-up notice from the post office. He leaned back into the vehicle and placed it conspicuously over the visor so he would see it when he left work. The one thing he did remember was the issue of *Defenders of Wildlife* magazine he had been meaning to bring to his office to show Hornman.

It wasn't until he got to his desk that he remembered he was having a birthday. This one, however, felt different from all the others birthdays since Samantha's death. Before, celebrations without her were out of the question. Now, he had the urge to have company again. He wanted to celebrate: he wanted to be with

Elizabeth. But she was in Montana and he in his Chicago office sitting at his desk waiting for his editor to arrive.

Reese glanced at a calendar and thought about how fast time passed since he worked on the wolf project in Idaho and Montana. The assignment was a success, and he was happy that he met Elizabeth English as a result of it, but the *Defenders* magazine article dampened his mood. When he heard David Hornman's voice from an adjoining room he, walked over to see him.

Entering the office, Reese shut the door and tossed the magazine on his editor's desk. Hornman had just hung up the telephone and swiveled his desk chair to face Reese. "Uh, oh" uttered Hornman as he stroked his shaved head with both hands. "Now what's bothering you?"

"Do you believe this is still going on? With federal officials like Gale Norton sabotaging the little protection these animals have, it won't be long before they're gone for good."

"Jeff, you're going to get us in trouble if you keep antagonizing these politicians."

"That's the problem. Everybody's afraid of the politicians, even the *Graphic*."

"Take it easy. Or do you want the old man to hear you?"

"Come on, Dave, just read the thing. I'm more worried about the fate of gray wolves than anything else."

Hornman read the blurb. He looked up at his pacing friend. "It's not going to end. You knew that when you returned from Stevensville."

"I know. It's happening everywhere. Minnesota has a pending bounty of a hundred and fifty bucks for a dead wolf. A hundred and fifty bucks! Do you believe it? I get sick when I hear this stuff."

"You've got to take it easy. You'll only get yourself an ulcer."

"I know, I know. I just can't help it," Reese said before turning to the other reason he was in Hornman's office. "I got a call yesterday afternoon from Charley Whittington. Remember him? He's the conservation guy who arranged for me to keep that wolf I had. He told me they picked up three poached wolf carcasses outside of Stevensville a few days ago."

Hornman rubbed the top of his head again. "That's disgusting! It's hard to believe this stuff still goes on."

"Not only that. He told me they're using poison to snuff out entire wolf families."

Hornman squirmed in his chair fiddling with a ballpoint pen. "There's not a hell of a lot anyone can do about this stupidity, pal. Hell, you wrote a book about this stuff. You did more than most."

"I want to do something else. I want to go up there and see what I can find out."

Hornman tossed the pen on his desk and stared at Reese. "To Stevensville? What for?"

Reese rubbed his hand across the back of his neck. "I've been in contact with Jacy Cayuse, that Indian kid. I phoned him last night and asked him to have a look at those three wolves to see if he could identify any of them. I'd like to go up and talk to him about it. Then I want to take a little hike up into Bass Creek."

"Nitika! You want to see about Nitika, don't you?"

"Yeah, her, too," Reese answered, his voice dropping off as he lowered his head. Reese also wanted to see Elizabeth English. He had mentioned her to Hornman before, but he didn't want to admit that she was another reason for him to go.

Hornman got up from his desk, poured a cup of water from the cooler and handed it to Reese. "Haven't you had enough pain up there? You lost your dog, you lost her pups and you see people still killing the wolves. Why go?"

Reese stared at Hornman. "I'll be back in a week."

Hornman groaned. "I suppose you'll want Friday off so you can get a head start, right?"

Reese felt himself smile for the first time all day. "Hey, you never know. There might be a piece in this for the magazine."

"I'll arrange everything. You can have as much time as you want," Hornman said as he watched his friend bolt for the door.

Reese left the office. He wanted to get home early to call Elizabeth. When he got into his Jeep, he saw the mail notice. He headed for the post office where he was surprised to be handed a large box.

Reese could feel his heart race when he saw the package was from Elizabeth. Though he had just spoken to her, the delivery reminded him of how much he missed her and he sped for home. The nine-mile drive through Cicero to his Westchester apartment was the fastest he had ever negotiated Chicago's heavy traffic. He thanked his luck to find a parking spot close to his walk-up, dashed from his car, raced through the vestibule and bounded up the single flight of stairs to his door.

Inside, he fumbled to open the package. Like the spark from a stun gun, shock bolted through Reese's chest as he pushed aside the tissue paper to reveal a beautiful saddle-colored parka. He removed the gift from the box and held it up. He checked the manufacturer's label: "Cabela's North Slope Goose Down Parka." He looked at the fabric examining the detail of the stitching. The coat was identical to the one he had gotten as a birthday present from Samantha seven years before.

Reese never told Elizabeth about Samantha's gift or that he buried it with Gretchen. That was his secret connection linking Samantha to Gretchen and he could not believe Elizabeth had bought him the same coat.

As he tried it on, he found an envelope tucked in a sleeve and opened it.

Dear Jeff: I hope this fits. I'm not so sure you will find use for it there, but when you come back to Montana, I know it will come in handy. I miss you so much. I wish we could celebrate together. I hope you have a wonderful birthday. Call me when you have a chance. Love, Beth

Reese's hand trembled as he dialed Elizabeth's number. Wearing the parka, he marveled at the gift and could not believe its timing. The phone rang several times and he became anxious for her to answer. When she did, he could barely contain himself. "Beth! I just opened your present. The parka," he blurted. "How on earth did you know?"

"You told me you were planning to get a coat. I don't remember you buying one while you were here, so…" She paused momentarily, "It's been a while. Did you already get one?"

"No, no. I needed one," Reese said as he realized the forethought of Elizabeth's present was incredible happenstance. He thought of trying to explain the remarkable coincidence, but quickly dismissed the impulse. "What a great gift, he said. One of the nicest presents I've ever gotten. And besides, this one will be good for when I get there. Thank you so much, Beth. I really love it."

"You're welcome. Happy birthday." More excitement filled Elizabeth's voice as Reese's words registered. "Did you decide when you're coming?"

"Beth, I couldn't sleep last night and I've given this a lot of thought."

Elizabeth noticed the changed tone of Jeff's call. "Would you come to Chicago?"

Shocked at the question, Elizabeth gulped. "To live?"

"No. No, I mean now. Tomorrow. You can catch an early flight. You could be here before noon."

A sudden fright stung into Elizabeth. "What about coming here? To Montana."

"I haven't changed my mind about that. I promised you, didn't I?"

"I thought you were coming to see about the wolf killings."

"I'm going to do that, too. Charley Whittington told me that he was preserving the wolves for evidence and that if I waited a while he might have a story for me after his investigation. I'm still going to come there. The only thing I've changed my mind about is when."

"I don't understand. You want me to come there?"

"Just for now," Reese pleaded. "Listen, I've got an idea. I've been putting off a business trip that I have to take to Canada. Do you still have your passport?"

"Yes. What's in Canada?"

"Wolves. Plenty of them. It'll be fun. What do you say?"

CHAPTER 28

"We humans fear the beast within the wolf because we do not understand the beast within ourselves."

- Gerald Hausman, *Meditations with Animals*

Elizabeth drove along the serpentine driveway out of Elk Woods, her thoughts boggled by the conflicts between joy and uncertainty. Her heart pounded; her mind raced. She thought about the whirlwind love affair between her and Reese culminating in his shocking proposal. She was convinced of her love for him, but after he told her about Samantha, Elizabeth wondered if his devotion to his deceased wife might sabotage his convictions to marry again.

Merging onto the highway toward the Missoula airport, Elizabeth tried to digest the magnitude of what had transpired within the last twenty-four hours. She had made plans the night before agreeing to fly to O'Hare to meet Reese. He told her to be prepared to spend the next few days with him on a business trip. If Reese intended to keep his promise to wed, she was willing to accept. The thought they would elope was exciting, and her pulse quickened at the daring idea.

As she entered the long-term parking lot of the terminal, Elizabeth shuddered thinking about her father's reaction. She would be gone for nearly a week before returning to Montana with Jeffrey Reese, a man whom John Dalton English considered an enemy at best. She thought about the devastating disappointments her father had suffered from her mother and brother, and now she was about to add more distress to an already troubled man. As difficult as it was, she loved her father. She also loved Jeff Reese, and the conflict so tangled her emotions that she began to cry.

While waiting at the boarding gate, she thought about her brother. She missed Jamie, but she did not miss the constant bickering between him and her father. She wondered whether Dalton would have been able to handle her mother's rejection better had Jamie not run off first. Elizabeth guessed that her father felt defeated by his son. In earlier years she had always seen strength in her father. Now, it appeared that Dalton had given up.

Had Jamie sat where she sat studying the departure times? There were so many cities and so many places where he could have gone. Did he board a plane just as she was about to, or did he hitch a ride? Despite having taken his entire bank account of nearly two hundred thousand dollars he earned working for his father, Jamie probably hitchhiked. "He was always a risk taker," Elizabeth said to herself. "He takes after mom."

During her flight, Elizabeth anguished about her father and his dealings with Martin Kerns. She attributed her father's vehemence against wolves to his association with Kerns. Dalton had no such hatred before meeting the vile man. It was as though her father became convinced that wolves were a threat to Elk Woods, the only love left for Dalton to hold on to after his son and wife were gone.

Her eyes grew heavy, but she fought not to close them, afraid of the recurring nightmare she had over hearing Kerns relate the pleasure he got from destroying wolves while he worked for Charles Whittington, a man whose job it was to protect them.

Reese was waiting for Elizabeth in the baggage claim area with the most delighted look she had ever seen on his face. Tears welled as she ran to his arms and clutched him tightly. She had never felt so safe or more loved as she held him close, her head to his chest listening to his heartbeat. Still hugging tightly, Reese hoisted her up and swung her gently around one full turn. He reached for her arms, transferred them to his shoulders so she could pull herself up to a long, passionate kiss.

Their embrace lingered and was the most fulfilling minute in Elizabeth's life. She was the first to release her hug, reaching for a Kleenex.

Reese searched through his pockets until he found two airline tickets. "These are for us."

Elizabeth looked up at him. "For Canada?"

"Yeah, I can't wait to see the wolves."

"Neither can I."

I hope you don't mind," Reese said. "I figured we'd do things a little differently. We can get married when we get back."

"The honeymoon before the wedding? I'll say that's different," Elizabeth laughed. "And I don't mind one bit," she said reaching up to kiss the man she loved with every part of her soul.

They talked as they got into Reese's car and drove out of the hectic airport. Reese held Elizabeth's hand. "I want you to meet my family before we go to Canada," he said. "That's why I insisted that you come to Chicago."

"Are they nearby?"

"They live in the town of Freeport, less than two hours from here. I'd like to drive out today if you're not too tired."

"No, I'm fine. But I'll be nervous about it."

"Why?"

"I'm a country girl. They're city folks. They may not like me."

"Impossible. Freeport is hardly a city. They'll like everything about you."

"Positive?"

"Positive. But what if you don't like them?"

"Impossible. I'll like everything about them."

"Positive?"

"Positively," Elizabeth said as they both broke into laughter at the same time.

"Then we'll see them later. It'll be a beginning for a great time, then off to Canada for a few days," said Reese with a fist pump.

After her smile faded, Elizabeth squeezed Reese's hand. "But what about your job? The wolves. What about the wolves?"

Reese pulled over to the curb and stopped the car. He did not want to be distracted by driving. "I haven't forgotten about them. I'll never forget about them. Charley Whittington is conducting an investigation to see if they can catch the poachers, and he said it might take a week or so before he has anything to go on, so I have some time. I called Jacy to ask him to hook up with Charley. Maybe he can help. There's not much I can do for a while, so I'll go back to Montana with you when we get back from Canada."

Elizabeth looked at Reese, her eyes locking on his. "Did you mention my father?"

"No, I didn't."

"Perhaps you should have."

"Beth, you don't know for sure that your father was responsible for those wolves. Let Whittington see what he can find out."

Turning to face Elizabeth, Reese reached for both her hands and held them firmly. "Look, we both need to get away from this for a while. This little trip will be the best thing we can do right now."

Determined not to allow the conversation to assault the day's good mood, Reese winked. "I've got another surprise," he said smiling.

Elizabeth could feel the charge of excitement from Reese. "More surprises? How much can a girl stand?"

"My book. It's being published. I've already received an advance."

Elizabeth's mouth opened wide to draw a deep breath and she shuddered her head. "My. That's good news. But I knew all along it was too good not to be considered. I'm so proud of you, Jeffrey Reese," she said reaching to clutch a fistful of shirt-collar and pulling him close enough to kiss.

"I don't know if I deserve all the accolades. If it wasn't for my boss pulling a few strings... You know, it helps to know a few people in the industry, but if it wasn't for you, I don't think any of it would have been possible," he said lifting her hand to his lips.

After toasting their excitement with a hug, Reese pulled into the main thoroughfare and merged with the traffic. "And while I was waiting for you this morning, I kept myself busy. Along with all my vacation time I've built up over the years, I put in for an extended leave of absence, so work isn't a problem, either."

"Tell me about Canada," Elizabeth said with that smile Reese loved so much.

"British Columbia, actually. My publishers are in Calgary. I've got to see them about some book cover designs. They want me to be photographed with a wolf."

"And me? Me, too?"

"If you behave yourself."

"I'll be as good as gold," she promised, her hands and fingertips forming a steeple to hide a grin.

Reese reached to lower her hands from her face. "When they called, they told me they could arrange a private seminar for us. It's a promotional thing to market the book. There's a wolf compound nearby that we'll visit. We'll be able to do something very few people get to do -- interact with the wolves. Touch them, be photographed with them and maybe you'll even be able to hold a wolf puppy."

"How great is that!" Elizabeth said, her excitement bursting like a child about to open the biggest birthday present she ever received.

* * *

Elizabeth watched the urban landscape slowly transform into forested countryside. "I'm surprised. We're not that far out of the city and it's already getting rural," she said.

Reese glanced over. "You like the open spaces, don't you?"

"I'm a country girl, remember?"

"I'm kind of partial to it myself. I grew up not far from here."

Suddenly, Elizabeth noticed a road sign. "Look, Jeff, there's a place called Loves Park. How romantic."

Reese grinned. "The name's deceiving. I know a place up the road that's a lot more romantic."

"I like romantic. Can we stop to see it?"

"I was hoping to," he said.

Twenty minutes later Reese turned off Route 75 onto a dirt road along the fast running waters of the Sugar River. When Elizabeth spotted the water, she got excited. "A trout stream?"

"You sure are a country girl," Reese said. "You see a brook and that's what you think about."

"Are there trout in it?"

"If there were, do you think you could catch more than I could?"

Elizabeth winked. "Remember the rule now. Whoever catches less, cleans."

"Ah, it's a good thing we don't have our rods and reels or *you'd* be cleaning fish," Reese said.

"That's not the way I recall how it went down the last time."

"One measly fish. Big deal!"

Elizabeth giggled. "I still think it's a good thing we don't have equipment."

"Yeah, it's a good thing."

They bumped along the dirt road for another half mile when an ivy-blanketed stone mill rose up and peeked out over a sylvan landscape. Alone, in a wild-flowered meadow, an ancient gristmill revealed itself and beckoned company. With a cedar-shingled roof so severely weathered, it no longer offered protection from the elements, the quaint structure had the charm of an old relic with an interesting history to relate.

"Is that the place you were talking about?" Elizabeth asked.

"Yeah. Neat, huh?"

"It's beautiful," she said. "Can we go inside?"

"I'll race you."

"You're on."

They got out, walked to meet in front of the car, and took a starter's stance. Elizabeth held up her hand. "Okay. On go. Ready--," she said as she took several quick strides and was running as fast as she could, "set---go!"

"Cheat!" Reese yelled as he ran to catch up. He chased her through knee high daisies and black-eyed Susans, and finally caught up as Elizabeth came to a low, river-rock wall. Reese held Elizabeth's hand as they gingerly scaled the stones, went into the tower-like structure, quickly climbed to the top and fell dizzily onto the planked flooring. Exhausted, they lay on their backs catching their breaths.

Elizabeth spoke first. "Do you realize this is the first time we've been truly alone?"

"We're not really alone." Reese pointed to a pair of mottled brown barn owls roosting on the rafters, their heads swiveled ninety degrees to peer at the couple.

Elizabeth looked up at the birds for a moment and then turned her attention to Reese and studied his face. Her heart beat musically within her and she whispered. "You have the nicest profile anyone could possibly imagine. I love it," she said tracing its contours with feathered fingers.

Reese warmed to her touch, gazed into sparkling eyes and found it difficult to express his feelings. He leaned toward Elizabeth, put his lips softly to her ear and yielded to his emotions. "You're amazing," he whispered. "There just are no other words to tell you how much you mean to me. I love you," he said as he touched his lips to hers.

Elizabeth swung her arms around Reese's neck and drew him into a crushing hug. "Listen. Can you hear my heart racing?" she asked.

Reese put his head to Elizabeth's chest and listened, but the beat of his own pulse muted the world around him. "My heart won't let me hear a thing."

Elizabeth's face glowed into a smile as she rested her head back on the wood flooring and looked up over Reese's shoulder at the owls. The birds had turned their heads away from the embracing couple as if to offer privacy. "I think we made the owls blush," she said. Do you think they'll mind if we make love in their tower?"

"No," he said liking her initiative. "They won't mind at all."

Elizabeth didn't realize how much he wanted that, too. They stayed in the gristmill for over an hour. The experience was tenderly sweet, emotional and one they both would never forget.

Back in the car, Elizabeth leaned over and kissed Reese on the cheek. "Was that a reward?" he asked.

"Yes. For bringing me here."

Reese couldn't keep from smiling. He felt lucky to have Elizabeth, and he was anxious to get to his parents' home to bring them the woman who brought his life back.

CHAPTER 29

"We believe that the last frail wonderful webs of wilderness are now vanishing from Earth."

- Lois Crisler, *Arctic Wild*

Receiving the call from Reese, Jacy made the four-hour trip on horseback directly to the conservation office to see Charley Whittington. He arrived at noon and as soon as he entered the building a feeling of discomfort grabbed at Jacy's stomach and churned it. He took a deep breath, removed his hat and combed back his hair with his fingers. Most indoor facilities seemed to have the same effect on the Indian, but government office buildings made him feel especially self-conscious.

Jacy was positive the uneasiness he felt as he walked into the vestibule had something to do with the assault to his sense of smell. Like walking into a library, the room had an odor he could never learn to appreciate. Smells of barns, horses and wet saddle leather were always less offensive than mildew, lingering tobacco, and stale air scents that now offended his nostrils as he entered the main office.

The short walk across the uninviting room seemed to take longer than it should have, and he tried to allow his imagination to transport him to a cedar grove back in the beloved foothills. He recollected the dewy fresh fragrance of a familiar fiddle fern thicket, closed his eyes and sniffed. But the threat to his senses grew more intense as he breathed in human body odor.

Slouched behind a crumb-infested desk, a bulky man strained in his chair to shift his weight as he picked at his neck and scratched. He swung lazily at flies swarming around a half-eaten pickle and squinted at the boy who approached him. Jacy stepped toward the desk as if nearing a funeral bier, spotted a nameplate and read the inscription to himself: “M. Kerns.”

“Mister Kerns, sir,” the boy said feeling the pierce of squinted eyes stab into him like poisoned arrows, “I came to see the game warden, Mister Charley.”

There was no response. Suddenly preoccupied with a more important task, the man examined a small scab he had scraped from the scaly skin beneath his folded chin. After inspecting the crusty debris clinging to his thumb, the man flicked it away with his index finger and returned his attention to the boy.

A lengthy glare froze Jacy’s nerve as he watched the hulk shift his feet from the desk to the floor, casually snip a fingernail with his teeth and then glance over his shoulder at the Regulator clock above a door that had Whittington’s name on it.

Jacy forced a smile hoping it might warm the clerk’s coldness. “Is Mister Charley here?”

“Ain’t nobody here by that name,” the man snapped as he spat a sliver of yellow fingernail at Jacy’s feet.

The smile slid away from Jacy’s face. He lifted his head, mustering as much pride as he could. “I come to see Mister Charley Whittington.”

“It’s Charles to you! Whata ya want wid him?”

“Mister Jeff Reese asked me to see him.”

“Sit down and wait. He’s busy,” growled the man as he inspected what remained of his dirty fingernails before glancing back at the Regulator.

Jacy, crushing his tattered hat in his hands, shuffled to a wooden bench near the door, sat and stared beyond it wishing he were outside. Aside from the wheeze of the clerk’s breathing, the only sound in the room was the old Regulator as it loudly ticked off twenty minutes before the door beneath it opened. Charles Whittington stepped from his office.

When Jacy saw Whittington look in his direction, the Indian rose to his feet immediately, tucked his hat behind his back, bowed his head and held the rigid posture of a peon in the presence of a master.

Jacy's obeisance did not go unnoticed, but it was not in Whittington's style to receive homage, so he gave Jacy a wink before speaking to the man at the desk. "Muzzy, I'm going to lunch. Want anything?"

"Yeah. Anything. Still hungry," he grumbled. "Oh, and that Injun kiddo there wants something from ya. But he'll wait 'til you get back from lunch."

Whittington walked over to the boy who still wrung his crumpled Stetson with both hands. "Hello there, Jacy? Were you waiting to see me?"

Jacy relaxed at Whittington's wink. "Yessir. But I don't want to take your lunch time Mister Charley."

"No problem. Been waiting long?"

"No sir," Jacy said wrinkling his brow to frown back at the desk clerk.

Whittington saw the glance and surmised that Kerns had been rude. He knew the man well, so he slung an arm around Jacy's shoulder as they stepped outside.

Whittington peered back to make certain that his clerk could not hear. "Jacy, you shouldn't pay Muzzy any mind. I know how he can be. His attitude is typical of some insignificant people who see themselves in a post they think is significant."

Jacy did not respond. Usually white men wouldn't say things about other white men, especially to an Indian. He just stared at Whittington until the man changed the subject.

"So, Mister Cayuse, you came to see me, did ya?"

"Yessir. Mister Jeffrey asked me to come to you. He asked me to look at the wolves that was killed by the ranchers."

Whittington glanced up at the sky, shook his head and then looked back at Jacy. "That's not a good idea."

"But Mister Jeff asked me," Jacy said nearly ripping his hat with his hands.

"I don't think you have to see them. I didn't have the heart to tell Mister Reese the truth when I spoke with him on the phone, but..." There was silence that screamed disgust before Whittington confessed. "One of them was the wolf he kept up at his place. The one you caught in your trap."

Jacy's voice trembled. "No, oh no. No, no. Are you sure, Mister Charley?"

Whittington couldn't look at the boy. "I'm sure," he said as he gazed off looking into emptiness on a busy street. "As soon as I saw him I thought he looked familiar. One look at his broken teeth and I was sure."

The news crushed Jacy's heart. "What about the others?"

"Look, we had to put the wolves in a freezer. My department is going to do an investigation to see if we can find out who killed them. I don't think it's a good idea for you to see them like that."

"No, please, Mister Charley. Please. I gotta see 'em for Mister Jeff. Please!"

Since he had already told Reese he would show the wolves to the boy, Whittington agreed. The identification, he thought, might help somehow. He knew that Jacy was the only one who may have seen the other wolves.

"It's not a pretty sight," Whittington said as he led Jacy around the building to a walk-in locker.

When Whittington opened the freezer, Jacy dropped to his knees. The young Indian had never felt a stab of pain go into his heart as he did then. The sight of the three wolves was more than the boy could stand and he rocked to and fro chanting in his native tongue.

There before Jacy, once noble animals, now stripped of all their dignity, Shako, the intelligent alpha female, Bartok, the fearless pack leader, and his loyal brother Dakota lay side by side by side in frozen death.

To Jacy, the ghastly dusting of frost over their stiffened bodies was a shroud of evil upon the deeds of man and he shook uncontrollably. Whittington writhed away from the scene, grasped the nape of his neck with both hands and tilted his head toward the ceiling. Jacy gagged on the choking lump in his throat, but did not cry.

CHAPTER 30

"There is little doubt that the wolf is the most adaptable animal, other than man, that the world has ever known."
- Douglas Pimlott, *The World of the Wolf*

Reese was in high spirits the morning after he and Elizabeth returned from visiting his parents. They were at his apartment preparing to leave for the photo shoot in Canada when the phone rang. When he heard Reese's voice, Jacy became emotional and fought valiantly to hold back sobs. "Mister Jeff, they killed him! They killed him, Mister Jeff. The *shon tonga*, it was Nitika's father. I saw him. He's dead, Mister Jeff. He's dead."

Reese squeezed the receiver as tightly as the message squeezed the spirit from his body, crushing his good mood like a giant gnarled fist had punched into his chest, grasped his heart and wrung it. It took a few moments before the words would come. "I - I know how you felt about that animal, Jay. I'm sorry. I'm really sorry."

Jacy felt guilty about Reese's apology. If anything, he thought it was he who owed an apology.

"Mister Jeff. Why did they have to kill those wolves? Those lobos never done nothin' wrong to nobody. Was it 'cause the pack was on their land?"

"No! No one owned that land. If anything, they were on land that should belong to them and all the other creatures of God's world."

"Then why, Mister Jeff, why?"

Reese could feel the boy's emotion pour through the phone. With his own anguish tearing at his insides, Reese searched for the right words and spoke as though giving a eulogy. "Son, the men who killed those wolves will never understand. Those people are much like the wolf."

Jacy shook his head from side to side; his eyes were about to erupt as he listened to his friend. Reese took a deep breath and tried to explain. "Humans and wolves evolved as group hunters. They depend upon the cooperation and caring of their own kind to survive. Like us, wolves take pleasure in companionship. They love touch and play and they're loyal to each other and devoted to their babies."

Reese knew he had Jacy's total attention, but he was unsure of the boy's comprehension. "But at the same time, wolves are individuals. Like men, they compete. And sometimes they try to eliminate their competition. Then they can be aggressive and violent. The men who killed those wolves thought of them as competition. They acted on an impulse that told them to eliminate what they saw as competitors."

Jacy was nearly inaudible. "Those men killed things just like themselves?"

Reese cringed at Jacy's question. The boy tried to grasp why the explanation forgave the unforgivable, and Reese struggled with the answer. "Yes. More or less. They've been doing it for a very long time. But I'm afraid the wolf has been doing it even longer."

"Men kill wolves, but wolves don't kill men, Mister Jeff. Do they?"

Hesitating before answering the question, Reese recalled what Jacy had told him of the death of his great-grandfather, a man murdered by settlers for releasing a snared wolf. Reese thought the boy could have asked a more difficult question - a question that a white man couldn't answer. Reese knew that Nez Perce Indians did not kill wolves. In fact, he knew of no Native Americans who hated, or ever even disliked wolves.

Reese was aware that slaughtering wolves was a white man's choice, borne of hatred and ignorance. For sure, Reese thought, the man for whom Jacy was named was hanged for an evil far more sinister than his disregard for Aryan conviction. Reese knew that it was his ancestors who held deeply-rooted hatred for the Indians, and he was aware the same misguided disdain was similar to that of the white man's despise for the wolf. And Reese was ashamed.

Jeffrey Reese shook his head as he paused to switch the phone from one ear to the other and finally answered. "No. No they don't, Jacy. That's one of the big differences between them and us."

A prolonged silence from the telephone, empty and cold, chilled Reese's heart. He thought about the wolf he nursed to health and wondered how difficult it was for it to return to its pack. He wondered about the relationship between it and the other slain wolves. Although he wished to know, he welcomed the mystery. It allowed him to imagine there was good in that portion of the wolf's life that he had helped to prolong. It was a consolation, however meager, but so necessary to abate the pain of Jacy's call.

Reese thought about Nitika and wondered if she lived. Here, the mystery was not so welcomed. Now, more than ever, he yearned to know. He knew Jacy, too, wanted to know.

Aching to do so, Reese shifted the direction of the conversation. "Jay, I want you to do something for me. Do you think you could find the wolf pack again like you did before?"

"Mister Jeff, I ain't bin back in the hills since Nitika went free, but I'm most sure I know where to find 'em. Do ya think Nitika is with the pack?"

"Well, there's only one way to find out, isn't there?"

Reese knew Jacy was smiling as the boy spoke. "When do you want to go, Mister Jeff?"

"I'm not going to be around for a few days. When I get back we'll go."

"You're goin' away Mister Jeff?"

"Mister Cayuse, my man, I'm planning to get married. But first I'm going on a short trip with Beth. As soon as I get back I'll call you."

"You gonna marry Miss Beth, Mister Jeff?

"I am. That is, if it's all right with you."

Jacy did not know what to say. Sometimes Reese said things Jacy didn't understand, so he thought of a safe response: "I like Miss Beth."

"Okay, then. Because, you know, if you didn't approve, I'd have to reconsider."

Jacy was silent for a moment as he thought about what Reese had just said. Again, the man confused him and he felt it would be better not to respond.

CHAPTER 31

"If the wolf is to survive, the wolf haters must be out numbered. They must be out shouted, out financed, outvoted. Finally their hate must be undone by a love for the whole of nature, for the unspoiled wilderness, and for the wolf as a beautiful, interesting and integral part of both."

- L. David Mech, *The Wolf*

After a three-hour flight from Calgary, the Boeing DC-10 made its final approach to O'Hare. Reese and Elizabeth sat in coach discussing their trip to Canada. "I had a great two days," Elizabeth said.

Reese reached for Elizabeth's hand. "I'm a little disappointed that you didn't get to hold a wolf pup."

"Just to be able to get as close as I did to the adults was awesome."

"When I put my hands on that big male…" Reese hesitated and gazed out the window at the river-like tarmac streaming up to meet the aircraft as it yawed slightly to adjust its confluence with the runway.

"I know," Elizabeth said. "I think I felt exactly what you were feeling. It was almost spiritual."

Reese turned his head from the window and stared into Elizabeth's eyes. "I got that same sensation the first time I touched the one I took care of, and when I heard them howl in the wild. It's hard to explain. Yes. Spiritual," he agreed.

"Kind of like satisfying a hunger," she said.

"Now that you mention it, I'm hungry. How about you?"

"You had to ask?"

"What do you say to grabbing a bite at the airport when we land."

"You had to ask?"

Reese laughed as the plane touched down and taxied toward gate 12. "I think we can get a sandwich at the food court."

"Do you think they'll have chicken sandwiches?"

"I wouldn't count on them being like yours."

"Then you'll order for both of us," Elizabeth insisted."

"In that case we're going to a place I know in town. They serve a great brunch. What do you say?"

"You had to ask?"

Reese smiled. "That's what I like about you. You're always ..."

"Hungry," she interrupted.

Reese's grin transformed into a laugh. "Yeah," he said. "That's what I like about you."

After the buffet brunch the couple went to Reese's apartment to change their clothes and repack before driving to Freeport to spend the last day with Reese's parents.

* * *

Maria, Reese's mother, couldn't help doting over the girl. The two women talked about many things, Jeff being the subject of most of their conversation. Although his devotion and his parent's love for Samantha never entered into their talks, the mention of Jeff's first wife could not be completely avoided. Elizabeth could see fret in the glistening brown of Maria's beautiful eyes, worry that her son's life would never be happy after he lost Samantha.

Reese's father adored Elizabeth, and whenever they were alone, Elizabeth's talks with Edward Reese were mostly geared to her interests.

"Jeff tells me you like wolves," Ed Reese said.

"Yeah, I think they're great, but I don't know of anyone who likes them more than Jeff does," Elizabeth said tilting her head, "except for Jacy Cayuse. Do you know Jacy?"

"We've never met, but Jeff told us much about the boy."

"How did Jeff become so interested in wolves? Did you and Mrs. Reese kindle it?"

Ed Reese chuckled, "Other than bringing him to New York City once when he was kid, we didn't have much to do with it."

"New York City got him interested in wolves?"

"When we took him to the Museum of Natural History it did."

"Oh? Tell me about that," Elizabeth said, "please."

"Not much to tell, really. I guess he was about nine years old, and there was an exhibit there that we could hardly pull him away from. Big glass enclosure with actual mounted animals, wolves trying to bring down a bull moose. The sight of that display with the wolves getting the worst of the fight was so realistic and impressive; Jeff just couldn't stop talking about it. He couldn't get over the size of the moose and he felt sorry for the wolves being trampled and tossed in the air. He saw the wolves as underdogs, I suppose, and since then he's always been interested in them."

Ed Reese lowered his glasses as he spoke, his blue eyes the outstanding features of a graciously aging face, weathered yet ruggedly handsome. "And you? How did you get to like wolves?"

"When I was a little girl I used to listen to them howling at night. I thought they sounded so sad. Then they disappeared and I missed hearing them. I've always felt bad that they were gone from Montana."

Before leaving their home, Elizabeth's warmth and charm had Maria and Ed Reese convinced that Jeff's life would be better for having Elizabeth English in it. It was a feeling that neither one thought they'd have after Samantha's death.

Maria begged her son to stay longer, but he refused. He was too preoccupied with getting back to Stevensville and the wolves.

* * *

The next day the couple flew to Montana where Elizabeth planned to drive to Elk Woods while Reese met with Jacy Cayuse to hike into the heart of the Bitterroots.

When their flight touched down in Missoula, Reese immediately contacted Jacy. "Hello Mister Jay, are you ready to do some hiking?"

"Mister Jeff! Hello! I'm all ready to go. Been waitin' for you."

"I'll meet you in Stevensville at the post office tomorrow morning. How early can you get there?"

"The sun won't be up yet, Mister Jeff."

"Good. I'm looking forward to it."

"Is Miss Beth gonna go, too?"

"Not this time, Jay. She's got a few things to take care of at home."

Early the next morning, Jeff Reese and his young companion headed for Bass Creek while Elizabeth planned to see her father.

Jacy was waiting for Reese when he and Elizabeth arrived at the post office in Stevensville a half-hour before sunrise. Elizabeth kissed Jeff goodbye and turned to Jacy. "Now don't let him get into any trouble, Jay. I'm counting on you to keep an eye on him for me."

Jacy was surprised when Elizabeth leaned toward him and kissed his forehead. He blushed as the sweetness of Shalimar filled his senses. He had never been that close to a white woman in his life, let alone being touched by one.

"I'll watch him today, Miss Beth. But you gotta watch him forever."

"Sounds like a plan, Mister Cayuse," she said as she hugged Reese one more time before saying another goodbye.

Elizabeth headed for Elk Woods. The excitement of her Chicago adventures and the pleasant memories of Reese's parents were behind her. Ahead lay the dreaded reality of what John Dalton English would do when she told him she was going to marry Jeffrey Reese.

This time she drove through the predawn more slowly than ever. Fixed on the headlamp beams cutting into the darkness, Elizabeth was watching for animals that might dart into her path. The drive reminded her of another slow ride she had taken many years before. As she got closer to Elk Woods, the recollection made her feel more comfortable about seeing Dalton, and her thoughts drifted to happier times.

A seven-year-old girl sat pressed against her dad watching the headlights of their pickup truck knife through the darkness. "Daddy, are we there yet?" she squealed.

"Not yet, Bethy. Not yet," the man said trying to calm his

daughter's excitement. "Another few minutes and we'll be at the river."

"Go faster, daddy. Go faster."

"What if a deer runs out? You wouldn't want me to hit a deer or a rabbit, would you?"

"No, no, daddy, no."

"Well if I drive too fast, we could hit one. Some animals run out at night, you know."

A short silence passed, but the girl's exhilaration would not allow her to be quiet. "Why doesn't Jamie like to go fishing, too?"

"Your brother never liked to go. He doesn't take to the outdoors like you do."

"I'll bet he don't like to dig worms."

"You don't seem to mind."

"That's part of the fun. Catching the bait is fun, too."

"Well, I don't know about that. All I know is that you always want to go with me when I go fishing. Jamie never wants to go hunting or fishing with me."

"I like fishin' better 'n hunting."

"I love them both, but I love my little girl more."

"I love fishin', too, but I love you more, too. Could we get married, daddy?"

Dalton contained a laugh as he put his arm around his daughter and pulled her close. "Well, now what would your mother do?

"Uh, well, she could marry Jamie."

"No, Bethy, mommy wouldn't want to be married to anybody but your old dad."

"Well, I'll just stay with you forever, then."

Elizabeth's reverie was broken when a burly raccoon trundled out of the brush into the road in front of her, but she had plenty of time to brake. She smiled as she watched the coon waddle into the blear of morning mist. "You're lucky J D taught me everything I know Mr. Racketty Coon, or you might have been squished," she said as she turned into the winding road toward Elk Woods.

After leaving the highway, the sheer beauty of the Bitterroot land sprawl revealed itself in the peach-blush of dawn. With each twist and turn of the half-mile drive from the main road, towering ponderosa pines yielded some of their taller predominance to smaller and more sparsely spaced conifers allowing glimpses of a distant, purplish mountainside. Vast stretches of emerald pastureland popped through the thinning tree line, and a rolling hillside lazily raised up to expose the soaring gateway of Elk Woods and its main driveway beyond.

Elizabeth could visualize the driveway before she got to it, a serpentine path of flat, brown, black and gray river-stone. The stone-roadway was one of her favorite features of the great ranch. No stone was cut or carved; instead each had a unique shape and had been strategically placed together like an interlocking jigsaw puzzle by a masonry artisan to become one blended surface of mottled colors leading to the portal of Elk Woods.

When she got out of her Blazer to open the twelve-foot wrought-iron gate as she had done countless times before, the morning song of a whippoorwill greeted the first tinge of daylight in the eastern sky, and the smell of cattle brought back more memories of her life at Elk Woods. She could see a little girl chasing after her twenty-year-old brother.

"Jamie! Jamie!" she squealed. "Where are ya going?"

James Atkins English stopped when he heard his nine-year-old sister calling and turned to face her. He shook his head as he examined the frown of the young girl's face and breathed a sigh. "No place."

"Why do you got that sack with you?"

"I just packed a few things. I'll be gone for a while."

"Where to? Where ya goin'? Can't I come, too?"

"No, Bethy, you can't because I don't know where I'm headed right now."

James was lying to his sister. He knew where he wanted to go, but telling his sister the truth would have been tantamount to telling his parents where he might be found, and that he wanted to avoid.

With what little he knew of his mother's affair, he could not explain to his young sister that he, like his mother, became disenchanted with Dalton English. Although he disapproved of her infidelity, he sympathized with Renee English who wanted to escape Elk Woods and her husband Dalton.

James averted his eyes from Elizabeth. "Look, Bethy, I just have to get away. I've got to get out of here."

"Why?" she asked without getting a response. "Don't go, Jamie."

"Bethy, you don't understand."

"Why? Why you goin' away?"

"Because I have to. Because dad is a chauvinistic capitalist. Do you know what that means?"

"No," she said with a shrug as she watched James trying to stuff shoulder-length hair under the back of a paisley red and yellow bandana tied to his forehead.

James hoisted a khaki-colored, canvas duffel bag decorated with blue and black peace signs, slung it over his shoulder, knelt by his sister and reached for her hand. "You're too small to understand, Bethy, but I can't take it here any more. The more dad and I argue, the worse it gets."

"How about mommy? Mommy don't yell at you."

"Listen. Say goodbye to mom for me, okay?"

The child realized she was failing to convince. "Mommy's not home now. Wait 'till she gets back home. Please!"

"No. If I do that I'll never get out of here."

"Mommy will cry and daddy will be mad if you go."

"He'll be happy. Trust me. Besides, he's got you. And you're special to him."

"When are you coming back?"

James stood up. "I'm not sure," he said as he leaned to kiss the top of his sister's head.

When James English turned to walk down the long, twisting drive out of Elk Woods that day, his sister did not know she would never see him again. He simply disappeared to embrace a movement that no longer existed. Having heard his father rail about the Hippies of the 1960s, James became engrossed in the history of the subculture applauding its politics and emulating the lifestyle Dalton detested. James irritated his father by calling himself a beatnik and a pacifist until the charade became an insurmountable obstacle between father and son. It was then that Dalton English began to drink more heavily.

When she entered the portal of the twenty-room house, more memories sprang from the thundering clang of the giant doors as she closed them behind her. As a child, Elizabeth never came into the house through those doors; they were simply too heavy for a little girl to close and she recalled having to lean with all of her weight to shut them. Now the sound banged off the marble flooring of the frescoed vestibule and resounded through the cavernous corridors echoing the emptiness that now resided there.

Elizabeth wended her way into the kitchen and sat at the seven-foot black granite table. She fingered the cold stone she used to call the "eating bench" where, as a little girl, she was pampered by servants and maids.

Dudley Bannister was the chief ranch hand on the vast acreage of Elk Woods and he knew Dalton very well. Even though his boss intimidated him, Bannister respected and liked Dalton more than any employee who ever worked at the big ranch. Dalton liked Bannister as well, and paid him far more money than a foreman could make on another ranch. Bannister's bank account grew beyond what the man could possibly spend, and it was loyalty that kept him working. Without any kin, he adopted the English family as his own and considered Dalton a formidable brother.

Except for old Bannister and a few of his men, all other help had been gone since Elizabeth's mother left Elk Woods. They were run off by Dalton and his too many alcoholic mood-swings nearly twenty years before. Since then, Elizabeth and the faithful, gentle-natured Bannister cared for Dalton and they became his only companions.

Elizabeth knew the time her father usually rose and she planned to surprise him with breakfast. Though he had stopped eating the meal years before, the memory of those mornings when she'd prepare all his food stirred her and she started a pot of coffee. Realizing Bannister sometimes cooked for her father, Elizabeth was happy to find the necessities in stock. She cooked a batch of pancakes and a slab of Canadian bacon she knew Dalton would not eat.

In much earlier years at Elk Woods, breakfast was the only meal Elizabeth's mother would attempt. Renee English was a poor cook, and when Dalton would sneak up to her as she fried breakfast sausage, he'd make James and Elizabeth laugh by teasing his wife. "Renee, are those chicken legs or frog eggs you're trying to harm?"

Elizabeth laughed to think how giggly she and her brother would get when Dalton did silly things. He was fun, and Elk Woods was fun back then, but that all changed when Renee English began her affair with a man in his mid twenties, nearly half her age, and Dalton's drinking turned into a serious problem.

Anxious for her father to come down from his second-floor bedroom, Elizabeth sat at the kitchen counter and gazed as far as she could see through a department-store-size picture window at the sunrise-reddening pastureland. She waited for nearly an hour sorry she hadn't gone with Jeff and Jacy.

She was thinking about Jeff, and feared for what he might discover. She thought about the wolves that were killed and hoped others survived. Although Reese would not talk of it, she knew he was concerned about Nitika and was likely the biggest reason for his excursion with Jacy. She prayed that Jeff not discover more heartbreak.

Elizabeth watched as the sun climbed above the bucolic vista before her, chasing the shadows from beneath great Ponderosa pines that, like tall sentinels, watched over the vast landscape of Elk Woods.

Miles away Reese and Jacy climbed into the foothills. There, the first warm rays of sunshine melted the dewdrops from the faces of rose-colored Pursch flowers, Jacobs ladder buds, and Pink Mountain heather.

"Look," Jacy said pointing to a sleek, red fox vixen as it emerged from a floral thicket. The men stood still, eyes fixed on the fox as it slinked along the shadows of a sassafras tree-line and hopped a stonewall returning to her den.

Jacy continued to lead the way, wading through a tide of goldenrod and waves of Queen Anne's lace. Puffs of milkweed seeds billowed up with the gentle breeze to form a halo over the landscape. Reese struggled to keep up, distracted by the profusion of wildflowers spraying their colors across the meadow to the line of yellow-green poplars accenting the foothills of the Bitterroot Mountains in summertime.

Reese's thoughts subdued the uplifting grandeur of the northwest. The three slain wolves were from the same pack he saw with Jacy when they made their last trip into the area. He was afraid of what he might find and two questions haunted him: What happened to the rest of that pack? Why were these leaders not with the others?

Reese remembered what Charley Whittington had told him about ranchers using strychnine and threatening to poison entire packs. That might explain why three wolves would travel out of their territory to where men could shoot them. Reese feared that he might discover an entire pack poisoned. His gut retched at the possibility and he began to dread that he had made the trip.

* * *

The aroma of coffee lured Dalton to the kitchen. When he saw his daughter, he staggered and reached for a wall to support himself. "Where the hell have you been all this time?"

"I phoned you about where I was going. Don't you remember?"

"Something about where your mother ran off to with her boy friend, was it?"

Elizabeth turned away to avoid her father's eyes. "Yes, I went to Canada, but not Montreal."

"Did you see her?"

"I just told you. I was nowhere near her."

"Who knows where the hell she is --- and who cares?"

Her mother was a subject Elizabeth wanted to avoid. "I fixed you something to eat. Would you like me to warm it?"

"Not hungry. Coffee. I'll have coffee."

Elizabeth got up to pour as Dalton crumpled into a chair. She set the cup down in front of her father and saw him look up at her expectantly. Elizabeth lowered her eyes as she spoke. "I suppose you want something for that."

"Sambuca."

"Why not take it as it is. You don't need anything in it."

Dalton glared at Elizabeth, mumbled under his breath and braced himself to rise. When he made an effort to get out of his chair, Elizabeth easily stopped him. "Stay there," she said disgustedly. "I'll get it."

Elizabeth handed her father the bottle and watched as he shakily poured the liqueur, overflowing his coffee cup and saucer, spilling the liquid onto the stone table. She took a fistful of paper napkins from the counter, pushed them toward her father and then sat at the table across from him. "Dad. I have to talk to you."

Dalton looked at his daughter, lifted the cup to his lips, took a sip of the now lukewarm coffee as if he expected it to be scalding and then nodded. "Speak," he said.

"I'm going to leave Elk Woods. I'm thinking of getting married."

Dalton was careful to put the cup down next to the filled saucer. Then he looked directly at Elizabeth and wrinkled his face. "You pregnant?"

Elizabeth took a deep breath as her eyes rolled up under their closing lids. After a long pause she answered. "No. I'm not," she said allowing her breath to escape and opening her eyes to a prolonged stare at her father.

"Who you marrying so fast?" he asked.

"Jeffrey Reese."

As though struck by a rattlesnake, Dalton reacted. His face whitened and his eyes blazed as he placed his left hand on the table for support, cocked his right arm as far back as he could and slapped his hand at the cup slamming it broken and splattering coffee into Elizabeth's waist. "You're a damned fool. Idiot!" he shouted. "Why him?"

Elizabeth burst into tears. "I fell in love, daddy."

"With a wolf kissing son-of-a ---. You don't have to get married to leave here. Just go."

"I'm not getting married to leave Elk Woods. I'm leaving Elk Woods to get married. I fell in love, or I would probably have stayed forever."

* * *

Four hours passed in silence as Reese and Jacy made their way deeper into the hills toward the bench that was once the home of wild wolves, when Jacy muffled a shout. "Mister Jeff, Mister Jeff. Look what I found," he said pointing to fresh wolf tracks. "Wolves are still here!"

When Reese looked at the tracks, his heart thumped like a grouse drumming on a hollow log. He hugged Jacy and found it difficult to whisper. "You're the best tracker in the Bitterroots. They're still here and you found them."

It didn't take long for the young Indian to read the signs and follow them closer to where a wolf pack had marked its territory. Stealthily, he crawled on hands and knees to the crest of a rise and peered over. Reese, a short distance behind, watched as Jacy motioned excitedly for him to come ahead. Jacy, gesturing for the binoculars, kept imploring Reese to hurry.

Reese dropped to his knees, crawled to Jacy and handed him the binoculars. Removing his hat, Reese peeked over the rise and squinted to see wolves basking in the midday heat several hundred yards away. He could feel his pulse quicken again as he counted six wolves sprawled in the sunshine, while a seventh kept vigil over the others. His heart raced at the sight of a healthy pack and he was glad he made the choice to find them.

"Jay, is that yellow one the same wolf we saw as a pup?" Reese whispered as he stared at Yuma with his golden coat glistening in the sun.

Jacy nodded as he handed Reese the binoculars. "Look, you can see his face. He looks like he's crying."

Reese, propped on his elbows, adjusted the focus and studied the wolf. "Those markings on his muzzle are called tear lines," he said. "Like a cheetah has."

"A cheater?" Jacy frowned.

"Cheetah," he laughed. It's an African cat. You know wolves don't cheat."

Jacy didn't answer. His heart thundered in his ears and he kept staring at the pack. Reese handed the boy the binoculars, rolled to his back and looked up into a deep blue sky. "Thanks," he whispered. --- "Thanks."

Reese stayed on his back and kept staring into the sky, watching cumulus clouds tumble into each other like puppies at play and he spoke softly to Jacy. "I think its time to get myself a puppy," he said. "Yes, Jay, I think it's time. Miss Beth will like that; don't you think?"

CHAPTER 32

"We cannot solve the problems we have created with the same thinking that created them."

- Albert Einstein

The rear portico to the Elk Woods mansion was nearly as huge as the front entranceway. Two, hand-tooled, elk-horn chairs guarded the oaken doorway with antler tines pointing downward like the sheathed sabers of Marine Corps sentries. Above, a twisting web of mule deer antlers sculpted into a large chandelier speared dim prongs of light upward into the darkness of the slate cupola over the big back porch. Dalton stretched his legs out as he leaned back in one of the chairs, arms folded across his chest watching Elizabeth as Bannister was helping her pack clothes into her SUV.

Elizabeth kept glancing toward her father expecting a reaction as she spoke to Bannister. "Dudley, I'll be in Stevensville at the motel for a few days," she said with side-glances at Dalton. "If you need me, you can reach me there. Otherwise I'll check back with you. Take care of him, okay?"

Anticipating his ire, Bannister sneaked a peek at Dalton in much the same way a beta wolf looks at his alpha brother. "Yes, Miss Beth, he'll be fine," said Bannister as he again glanced at Dalton expecting to be redressed.

Dalton raised his voice. "Don't talk as if I wasn't here. Either of you! I can take care of myself."

Bannister bristled at Dalton's shout, looked at Elizabeth and swiveled glances between her and his boss before quick-stepping it for the sanctuary of the bunkhouse. Elizabeth stopped packing and went to her father's side. She knelt by his chair and reached for his trembling hand and examined it. She thought how different they looked from when she was a child. Then, bluish veins were prominent on the back of his hand, and she recalled fingering the vessels to feel a resisting pulse deliver its wealthy freight. Now, no longer visible beneath weathered skin, the veins relaxed, their cargo diluted by alcohol. "I am worried about you. You do know that, don't you?"

Dalton pulled his hand from his daughter's grasp. "I'm not helpless. I've been able to take care of myself for a long time."

"The ranch might be getting to be a bit much," Elizabeth said with a glance in the direction of Bannister as he scampered into the shadows toward the bunkhouse.

Dalton glared at Elizabeth. "This place doesn't need that much. I just have to keep the wolves at bay."

Elizabeth rose to her feet. "Daddy. There's something I need to know and I want you to be honest with me. Did you have anything to do with the three dead wolves they have down in Stevensville? They were shot over a week ago."

"What are you talking about?"

"Jeff Reese told me they're preserving three wolves that were poached. They're trying to find out who killed them. Did you have anything to do with it?"

"I thought I told you to mind your own business about my affairs!" Dalton shouted.

Dalton looked down at the ground. He was familiar with the serious edge Elizabeth's words could take and he prepared himself as she spoke. "You did. Didn't you? You put that Kerns man up to it. Didn't you, J D?"

Dalton squirmed and raised his head to glare at his daughter. "What if I did? So what. Who cares about those vermin?"

"I care. Jeff Reese cares. And, it wasn't that long ago that Dudley asked me why you disliked them so much. There are a lot of us who care. People are starting to know better than to destroy them."

"I don't give a rat's rear end who cares. They don't know any better. But, you? You care? That's the limit!"

"It's against the law, J D. They're looking for the people who did that."

Dalton's face reddened, the veins in his neck protruding ominously. "What are you going to do? Turn me in? Yeah, Muzzy did it. I paid him to do it. He was going up to poison the den and the stupid things were trying to protect it. Shot one, and the others just stood there, so he shot all three. He'd a'killed the whole pack, but they ran off. Too bad he couldn't kill 'em all. Only got the dumb ones."

Elizabeth watched as Dalton struggled to rise from his chair, his eyes burning into her. A peculiar feeling tumbled in her chest; the sensation was unexpected and it caught her by surprise. Of all the emotions she experienced with Dalton, the only one she never felt was guilt.

As a little girl, she knew the excited joy of her father's love when she caught her first trout. She shuddered in fear of his anger tantrums toward her brother and was despondent for his sorrow and the drinking that her mother helped bring into his life. And there were times when she hated everything about him, but guilt was a new emotion for her and it made her follow him into the house, through the halls and to his office. She did not enter; the room was his sanctuary and she always respected that.

Dalton ambled to his desk, crashed down into the chair, grabbed the phone and dialed the number for the conservation office. Martin Kerns answered the call. "DEC, Kerns here."

"Is Whittington there?"

Dalton's tone was angry and Kerns recognized the man's voice. Startled that Dalton had called him at his work, Kerns snarled into the receiver. "Why you callin' here J D?"

"To talk to you. Can your boss hear you?"

"No. He ain't around."

"Too bad, maybe I *should* talk to him."

"Whatta ya want J D?"

As he spoke, Dalton lanced an uninterrupted, metallic stare across the room at Elizabeth standing in the doorway. "Muzzy, what happened with those wolves you showed me at the ranch?"

"Whittington froze 'em."

"How in the name of Hell did he get them?"

"I brung 'em here. I wanted the skins."

"The skins? You wanted the pelts?"

"Yeah, there's money in wolf hides."

Dalton looked away from Elizabeth. "I paid you to get rid of them, and you bring them to your office? Are you a complete idiot? Whittington's going to find out you killed them."

"No, he ain't. I told him I found them shot. He don't know nuthin."

"Elizabeth knows, for Chrissake, and so does Jeffrey Reese!"

"Who's that?"

"You ass. If you ever read anything in your whole freakin' life you'd know." Dalton glanced back at Elizabeth. "He's a writer. He thinks he's going to save the goddamned wolves."

"So what!"

"So what? He can expose you. That's what!"

"How?"

"You kept the evidence, you moron. To get a few bucks for three mangy pelts, you screwed up. You're finished. You screwed up everything."

Kerns was silent for a moment before responding. "Uh - hu -- how about you? If- if he squeals and I get in trouble; so will you."

"No one's going to fire me, you jackass. But you're going to lose your lousy little job."

The gasps of heavy breathing were the only interruptions to another long silence before Kerns said: "Get - uh, get Elizabeth to - to - talk to him. Tell your daughter to - to help."

Dalton leaned back in his chair and laughed. "Now that's one of the funniest things I've heard since I kicked the slats out of my cradle after I heard my first joke. She's standing right here. Would you like to try telling her?"

Kerns began to whine. "I'll lose my pension. Thirty years of work and I'll lose everything. What'll I do?"

Dalton snickered. "I sure hope you can sell those pelts, Muzzy."

"If I lose my job, ya gotta help me, J D. I can work. I-- I know about cows 'n' stuff. I can work for you."

Dalton's hiss was deliberately slow. "If you ever set one hair of your fat ass on my ranch again, I'll shoot you. In fact, if I had only one bullet and you and a wolf were to come anywhere near my property at the same time, the wolf would be the only one to make it back to its hole in the ground for dinner."

Dalton slammed down the receiver and looked up at his daughter. "I'll call Charley Whittington tomorrow. I'll tell him everything."

Still standing in the doorway, Elizabeth shot a hand to her mouth to stifle words she wanted to say to Dalton. She wanted to tell him he did the right thing. She wanted to hug him and say that everything would be fine, that all wolves would be better for what he did. She wanted to tell him that his ire toward wolves was displacement for the anger he held toward her mother.

For years Elizabeth knew Dalton blamed himself for losing the woman he loved so much. Elk Woods became Dalton's life and he would not allow it another loss lest he see himself as less of a man. Elizabeth always knew he had been trying to protect Elk Woods from losing anything, not one steer, not one single calf, and thus wolves became Dalton's enemies. Elizabeth wanted to tell her father that he had finally conquered his demons. She wanted to say how proud she was to be his daughter. But she didn't.

She watched her father strain to get out of his chair, but slouch back down as though the effort wasn't worth it. Dalton bowed his head for a moment and then looked up to motion his daughter to him. "Sit down," he said. "I want to talk to you."

Expecting a lecture, Elizabeth walked into the room and sat before him. "Daddy, Muzzy is a bad man."

"Muzzy is a stupid man, and I can't have stupid people working for me."

"You've got Dudley. You don't need people to kill wolves."

"Kerns is history. I'll call Charley Whittington after you leave."

"Won't you get in trouble, too? They'll have a hearing or something, won't they?"

"What do I care about that? What'll they do, fine me? Big freakin' deal. Muzzy was stupid."

"Is that the only reason you're turning Kerns in? Because he's stupid?"

"You were right about him. What else do you want?"

"I'm right about the wolves, too. There's a lot more to them than you think."

"Don't go crazy on me now, Mary Poppins. There's not enough sugar in the world to make me swallow that medicine. There's only so much I can take in one day, for Chrissake. I've surrounded myself with morons. I'm sick of it."

"Does that include me?"

"You're marrying a wolf kisser, aren't you?"

"You should be happy for me. I found someone I love."

Dalton stared at Elizabeth, silent for moments that lingered in pain. "Does he…love you?" he asked somberly.

"Yes. He loves me."

John Dalton English felt his pulse quicken. His mind wrestled an internal battle. He expected anger, ugly and searing, to charge in with a thirst for rage that alcohol alone could quench. Instead he felt warmth spread into his being, calm and soothing, and he identified joy, that long-forgotten emotion melding with sadness.

Elizabeth thought she saw Dalton tear up. "You okay, dad?"

Dalton swallowed hard. "Bethy, I know I've neglected you since your mother left. You've had to put up with my temper, but I want you to know it was never about you. You're the only one who stuck by me. You're the only one who loved me enough to stay with me even when the booze took over."

Elizabeth tried to stop her father, but he shook his head. "No, it's true." He said. "Here you have someone who loves you, and I'm thinking about myself instead of being happy for you. Are you sure he loves you?"

"Yes. I'm certain of it."

Dalton's eyes, tearing by that realization, searched his daughter's face. "Then I'm glad for you because now you've got two guys loving you." He dragged the fingers of his right hand across the nape of his neck. "And don't screw it up," he said regaining his composure with the tight-lipped grin.

"You haven't told me you loved me since I was a little girl. Why was that so hard to say?"

"Dalton looked away. "Now I *know* I need a drink."

"No. Answer my question," she said as she got up and went to her father's side, kneeled and reached for his hand. "Why couldn't you say it before?"

Dalton put his hand over hers. "Your hands are cold."

Elizabeth nodded. "They're always cold. You know that."

When Elizabeth held her stare, Dalton realized he had to answer. He took her hand in his and rubbed it gently. "Anyone I've ever cared about has run out on me. I was afraid the day would come when you'd leave, too."

"But I'm not running out on you. I'm going to get married. You want me to be happy, don't you?"

Dalton's eyes were fixed on his daughter; only his head moved with a slight nod.

Elizabeth rose, urged her father from his chair and put her arms around him. "Then I'm going to be very happy. You said so."

Dalton hugged her back. He held the embrace savoring his daughter's touch for as long as his serious side would allow. "Does that mean I have to have that Reese guy around here now? I told you I'm sick of morons," he said gently pulling from his daughter's arms with an attempt to wrinkle his brow and mouth into a frown. But when he saw Elizabeth's smirk, it ironed the lines of his face and reformed them into a huge smile.

Elizabeth winked at her father and changed the subject. "Daddy, can I make dinner for you before I leave?"

Dalton's face lit up again. "If I let you cook dinner, will you have a cocktail with me first?"

Elizabeth didn't answer him and when she pursed her lips, Dalton reacted. "Okay, okay," he said. "No booze ---- until you leave."

"Daddy," Elizabeth said, her eyes dancing, "as long as you're in an agreeable mood, will you do something else for me?"

Dalton exaggerated gritting his teeth. "Now what am I in for?"

"I want you to read something."

Dalton cocked his head and narrowed his eyes. "What?"

"Jeff Reese wrote a book. I want you to read it."

Dalton's jaw slacked spreading incredulity across his face. "About wolves?"

"Yes, it's about wolves."

Dalton stared at his daughter for a moment and then glanced over at his collection of books. "Well I'll be damned," he grimaced. "Talk about having wolves at your door; now she wants the damned things in my library. I'll have to think about that, --- Miss Lizzy."

"Get some rest, --- Mister J D. I'll be in the kitchen. Call me if you need me.

CHAPTER 33

"Held within a wolf's gaze has been everything I've needed to keep alive my sense of connection to the earth."
- Douglas W. Smith, *Decade of the Wolf*

Reese lay gazing into the sky. The world around him had taken on a new perspective, for heaven itself seemed visible through the silvery clouds. He was reclining in Eden's vestibule about to be invited into her inner domain. There was a peaceful feeling within his chest that swelled from his heart and pulsed a glow of warmth about his entire body. He wanted this good feeling to continue, so he thought about Elizabeth, hoping she was having as much luck as he when Jacy mumbled something that Reese couldn't understand.

Jeff rolled back on his stomach and propped himself up again to look at Jacy. The boy seemed shocked. His jaw hung limp and he couldn't speak. Reese studied the Indian's face stricken in a slack-jawed mask of disbelief.

"What is it?" Reese asked as he nudged the boy and reached for the binoculars.

Still Jacy did not answer. The Indian groped for the binoculars hanging from his neck and clumsily offered them toward Reese without looking away from that which put him into a speechless trance.

Reese fumbled with the binoculars. Anxious to see what it was that shocked Jacy, clumsy fingers fiddled with the glasses as he raised them to his eyes. Reese peered through the binoculars, lowering them several times while keeping his stare on the distant sight. Thinking the instrument had malfunctioned, Reese fought with the focus wheel. Again he raised the binoculars to his eyes. The animal he was trying to look at was now in sharp focus. From behind Yuma, into the brilliant sunlight, a miracle appeared and Reese lost his breath. Nitika came into view.

Reese gulped for air and it clogged in his throat. He watched in awe as she led three frisky pups out of the den to Yuma's side. His vision blurred momentarily until he knuckled tears from his eyes and then continued to look at Nitika.

He managed to breathe a whisper to Jacy. "She's awesome!"

Jacy gushed back. "She made it Mister Jeff, she made it. And she got pups! See 'em?"

"Yeah, Jay. I see them. They look just like Nitika. Just like her."

A warm, peaceful feeling overcame Jeffrey Reese as he watched the puppies gambol about Nitika and Yuma, playfully tumbling and wrestling with one another. He thought about Gretchen and he knew that a part of her was there and it made him feel good.

Jacy and Reese shared the binoculars, watching the pack for nearly an hour. It was evident the yellow wolf was the leader. The wolves of his troop showed him the most respect, and only the pups received more affection.

"Mister Jeff, I was wrong about Nitika. She's an alpha. An alpha wolf-dog."

"Maybe so, my man. But I think that gold-colored wolf she has for a mate had something to do with it."

"Why did an alpha lobo take a mate that's part dog?"

"I don't know, pal. I never thought anything like that was even possible. I wish I knew how she got accepted into that pack, but I'm glad she did. I -- I'm totally surprised, but I'm really glad she did."

After watching the pack for the rest of the afternoon, Reese finally turned to Jacy. "I think we have to leave these guys to their lives, Jay. It's time to go."

Reluctantly, Jacy nodded. He labored to his feet and glanced at Reese and then at the wolves. The boy was wrestling with his thoughts, and Reese sensed it.

"I don't want to leave, either," Reese said.

"It's not that, Mister Jeff. I was just hopin'…" The boy's voice trailed off.

"What is it, Jay? What would you like to do?" Reese asked, his feelings for the boy apparent in the pathos of his tone.

"I want to call her. I want to call to Nitika."

Jeff Reese was never more skeptical of anything in his life, but he would not let on to Jacy. "Give her a shout, son. I was thinking of doing that myself," he fibbed.

Jacy smiled at Reese, turned, cupped his hands to his mouth and called. "Nitikaaaah! Nitikaaaah! Nitikaaaaaaah!"

Reese lifted his binoculars, concentrating them on Nitika and saw her become alert and look in his direction. In complete amazement, he watched her take several steps forward, stop and gaze up at the ridge, her ears pitched forward in total concentration.

Turning to Jacy, Reese whispered: "Jay, call once more."

When Jacy called her name again, Nitika started to walk toward them, but Yuma blocked her path. The big wolf seemed to be trying to keep her from getting by, but Nitika was persistent and kept nudging to get past her mate. Once more Jacy called, and once more Nitika responded. She dodged past Yuma and trotted toward the ridge, toward Jacy and Reese; Yuma followed close behind her.

Reese could not believe what he was seeing. "She's coming. She's coming," he choked the words out. "I can't believe she's trying to come to you, Jay."

At a steady trot, Nitika headed for the rise. Yuma turned momentarily to chase the three pups back to the den where a diminutive, light-colored wolf greeted them. Then Yuma broke into a lope to catch up to Nitika.

In a few moments Nitika reached the rise where she slowed her pace. With every hair on his mane bristling, Yuma slinked to a crawl behind her, his eyes fixed, his ears slanted downward, his nose twitching and quivering, testing the air. The sights, sounds and smells, though incomprehensible to the wolf, were familiar to Nitika. Something deep within the wolf made it keenly distrust these unfamiliar creatures.

A deep breath gushed from Yuma's lungs rumbling to a low growl in his throat before turning into a sound that more resembled a yelp than a bark, but the attempts to call Nitika were futile. She continued a hesitant walk closer and closer to Jacy. Yuma stayed behind, several yards back. Curled high exposing formidable canine teeth, his upper muzzle vibrated to a deep, ominous snarl.

Jacy stooped, patting his knee. His voice cracked as he softly called. "Come Nitika. Come. C'mon girl. C'mon."

Reese, in a frozen trance, watched as Nitika wagged her tail and extended her nose to Jacy's hand. Yuma would not come closer. He stayed away, staring at Nitika and continued growling lowly at the two strange beings.

When Jacy reached to touch Nitika, Yuma became furious and made a mock attack toward Jacy, but Nitika turned to go to her mate and calmed him with affection, licking at his muzzle. When Yuma sat back on his haunches, Nitika turned and sauntered to Jacy.

At the touch of her coat, a sensation coursed through the boy's chest and embraced his heart. The feeling seemed to pause momentarily before rushing up into his throat where it choked a spasm that surged further upward and welled into his eyes. The wave of emotion was so intense that it flooded Jacy's soul and then poured forth. For the first time since his childhood, tears overflowed and ran down Jacy Cayuse's face onto Nitika's muzzle. A taste of the salty fluid had Nitika licking the boy's face with her velvet tongue.

Reese kneeled down and took in the miraculous spectacle. Nitika rolled on her back and allowed Jacy to rub her chest for several seconds and then she stood up and looked directly at Reese.

Reese was awestruck as Nitika strode to him and nuzzled his extended hand. He ran his open palm over her head and down her shoulders to her back. Nitika's black roan saddle resembled Gretchen's and its warmth rekindled fond memories as Reese sank his fingers into the luxuriant fur. The man stroked the side of Nitika's muzzle and brushed his hand to her ears and rubbed them. Her reaction was exactly like Gretchen's and Reese gulped deeply trying to suppress the tears welling in his eyes.

Spellbound, as if suspended in a trance, Reese and Jacy watched Nitika slowly back away from Reese's touch, turn and amble to her mate's side. Without taking his stare from Reese, Yuma sniffed curiously at Nitika. The alpha wolf growled softly as he drew in the odor of man for the first time in his life. Secretly, Reese hoped the wolf would never again have to know the scent as he watched both animals turn to rejoin the pack and their pups.

Without a backward glance, Nitika broke into a trot and led her mate toward the den site. It was Yuma who stopped. He turned to take a last look at the two men, his sulfur eyes fixed on them in a long lupine gaze. The stare penetrated into Jeffrey Reese's soul stirring a mysterious urge to follow this unfettered creature, defiantly proud and free. It was a gaze that Reese would feel forever piercing into his psyche forging an indelible connection to the wild.

Despite the sophistication of her body language and the multiple meanings of her vocalizations, Nitika could not tell Yuma about her past association with these strange creatures she greeted like members of her pack. Yuma and his wolves would never know these men were responsible for her ever being among people. What mattered to Yuma and his wolves was that Nitika was the alpha female and that she was with them.

Once again, the wolves were reunited and that was all that mattered to any of them.

Epilogue

"They seem to possess so many qualities we admire, but one above all resonates strongest, knowing all that has befallen them at the hands of man. Wolves forgive."

- Jamie Dutcher, *Wolves at Our Door*

No spirit or wraith lives beyond its charge. When the last inhabitants of the Earth perish, my wolves will have been gone eons before, and I, too, will have expired with them. Among the billions of canids to have lived, all have stories that I know, but none that I have told save those of Bartok's clan.

Now that my tale of Anoki, Shako and Yuma is done, I have other wolves to tend, but let there be closure to Nitika, Dakota and the humans they have known.

One year after my story, Jacy Cayuse nearly lost his life. He spent three days in a Billings hospital, the result of a severe beating by two hunting outfitters when he railed against their claims that wolves decimated the elk herd beyond the borders of Yellowstone National Park. *The Montanian Gazette* reported the attack on the "Nez Perce militant" had more to do with the "audacity of an Indian to challenge local hunting guides" than it did about their charges that wolves were responsible for their loss of revenue.

Jacy left the Nez Perce tribal lands for good when he was nineteen. With the help of Jeffrey Reese and Charley Whittington, Jacy got a job working for the U.S. Fish and Wildlife Service where he became involved with relocation projects for the red wolf in New Mexico. Jacy's work also took him to Alaska, Michigan and

Minnesota where he could do what he loved best: study and work with gray wolves in the wild.

Martin (Muzzy) Kerns maintained his innocence during a three-day hearing of the Montana Wildlife Service. Found to have violated departmental regulations mainly due to the testimony of Charles Whittington and John Dalton English, Kern's position was terminated and his pension with the Montana Department of Conservation canceled indefinitely. Kerns was later tried by the State of Montana for poaching wolves and endangering wildlife. He was found guilty and sentenced to eighteen months in prison and fined $20,000.

Due to his cooperation and testimony at the Kerns hearing, Dalton English wasn't charged for his complicity in poaching wolves in the Bitterroot Mountains. Two years after Elizabeth moved from his Elk Woods ranch, Dalton died. The official cause of death was listed as sclerosis. Some attributed his demise to his daughter's departure, but that was not true. He spoke with Elizabeth many times and she took great pleasure in hearing his praise of Reese's book. Dalton English's entire estate was uncontested and left to his daughter.

Elizabeth searched unsuccessfully for her brother James in hope of sharing her inheritance. She had returned to Elk Woods to visit with her father many times before his death, but in deference to Dalton, she always went without Reese.

Jeffrey Reese never returned to his job with *The National Graphic*. He married Elizabeth, and later began work on his second novel. After the Elk Woods estate was sold, the couple bought a small ranch along the banks of the Gallatin River in the magnificent Big Sky area of Montana where their Alaskan malamute puppy had plenty of space to run and play. There he and Elizabeth fished for trout and enjoyed the prime years of their lives together.

Yuma, like his father Bartok, became the heart and soul of his pack. With the threat of wolf haters ever increasing, the alpha would lead his wolves out of the Bitterroots to a safer home closer to the Canadian border. The golden wolf lived for seven more years in absolute dedication to his mate and pack before he died. Yuma was nearly eleven-years-old at the time of his death, a remarkable longevity for a wolf in the wild.

In Nitika's lifetime she successfully raised four litters of pups. Without Yuma, the pack, disoriented for loss of a leader, left the densite and dispersed into splinter groups. But Nitika would not leave her mate. Refusing to eat or drink, the alpha female died at Yuma's side within ten days of the golden wolf's passing.

* * *

In 2006, Alaskan governor, Frank Murkowski allowed trophy hunters to gun down wolves from airplanes or run them to exhaustion with snowmobiles and shoot them point blank. Since the 1995 Yellowstone wolf recovery project, wolf haters in the park's immediate vicinity have illegally slaughtered thirty wolves. In Idaho, the deadly poison 1080 was being used to kill entire packs, the direct result of the Idaho legislature's voting to remove all wolves from the state – a certain sentence of doom for one of earth's most magnificent predators.

In February of 2008, the federal government removed the gray wolf from its protection under the endangered species list. They still persist: those who will shoot and poison the last of the wolves into oblivion. For some, the journey across the great expanse of misunderstanding has not yet begun.

Author's Note

Looking upon one of the last wolves in Mexico to be killed, famed naturalist Aldo Leopold recounted: "*We reached the old wolf in time to watch a fierce green fire dying in her eyes.*"

My inspiration for *Cry Wolf, Cry* came from a very brief horrific scene. Nature and animals have always held a fascination for me, and one evening as I worked the TV remote scanning the channels, I caught the last moments of what may have been a wolf documentary.

As credits rolled at the program's end, I saw only the final seconds of a wolf's life. A magnificent timber wolf, its forepaw crushed in a steel trap, struggled for its life. The image of that hapless animal cowering, pulling away with all its strength as it looked up at its executioner, haunted me. I imagined the animal's thoughts; I sensed its fear; I felt its pain.

Lupine eyes, widened in panic, followed the movement of a rifle's muzzle lowering to the wolf's breast. Eyes that pleaded for mercy flinched shut at the weapon's blast, and then opened slowly with a distant stare of resignation as the life of the wolf extinguished from its quivering body. The eyes of that wolf remained open even in death, and as those soulful, yellow-green eyes lost their fire, my emotions for a wild animal were tried like never before.

In desperation I looked for a newspaper, a TV guide; I reviewed the channels trying to find reason for what I had seen, but I was unable track a source. As determined as I was enraged, I began a search. In an attempt to put a semblance of sense to an act I found totally incomprehensible, my research intrigued me deeply into the world of the wolf.

What I learned was illuminating. What I discovered, fascinating, and I yearned to share my education about the gray wolf with the writing of *Cry Wolf, Cry*.

Bibliography

Askins, Renee. *Shadow Mountain.* New York: Doubleday, 2002.

Ballantine, Richard & Jim Dutcher. *The Sawtooth Wolves.* Bearsville, New York: Rufus Publications, Inc., 1996.

Bangs, Ed. *Return of a Predator*: *Wolf Recovery in Montana*. Helena, Mt.: United States Fish and Wildlife Service (USFWS), 1991.

Barry, Scott Ian. *Wolf Empire*. Guilford, Ct.: The Lyons Press, 2007.

Bass, Rick. *The Ninemile Wolves*. Livingston, Mt.: Clark City Press, 1993.

Beston, Henry. *The Outrmost House*. New York: Doubleday & Doran, 1928.

Bush, Robert H. *The Wolf Almanac*. Guilford, Ct.: The Lyons Press, 1995.

Crisler, Lois. *Arctic Wild.* New York: Harper Collins, 1958.

Durell, Gerald M. *Beasts in My Belfry*. London: Book Club Associates, 1973.

Dutcher, Jim & Jamie Dutcher. *Wolves at Our Door*. New York: Touchstone Books/Simon & Schuster, 2002.

Ellis, Shaun & Monty Sloan. *Spirit of the Wolf.* New York: Paragon Books/Barnes & Noble, 2006.

Halfpenny, James C. *Yellowstone Wolves In the Wild.* Helena, Mt.: Riverhead Publishing, 2003.

Hausman, Gerald. *Meditations with Animals*. Rochester, Vt.: Inner Traditions, 1986.

Jans, Nick. *Alaska.* Canada: Sasquatch Press. 2002.

Kipling, Rudyard, *The Jungle Book.* New York: MacMillan Press, 1894.

Leopold, Aldo. *A Sand County Almanac*. New York: Oxford University Press, 1949.

Lopez, Barry H. *Of Wolves and Men*. New York: Charles Scribner's Sons, 1978.

Lorenz, Konrad. *King Solomon's Ring*. New York: Thomas Y. Crowell Company, Inc., 1952.

McBride, Chris. *The White Lions of Timbavati*. London: Padding Press Ltd., 1977.

McIntire, Rick. *The War Against the Wolf.* Stillwater, Minn.: Voyager Press, 1995.

Mech, L. David. *The Wolf.* Stillwater, Minn.: University of Minnesota Press, 1970.

Menatory, Anne. *The Art of Being a Wolf.* New York: Barnes & Noble, 2007.

Mowat, Farley. *Never Cry Wolf.* Toronto, Canada: McClelland & Stewart, 1963.

Phillips, Michael K. & Douglas W. Smith. *The Wolves of Yellowstone*. New York: Vintage Books/Random House, 1996.

Rutter, Russell J. & Douglas H. Pimlott. *The world of the Wolf.* Philadelphia & New York: J. B. Lippincott Company, 1968.

Smith, Douglas W. & Ferguson, Gary. *Decade Of the Wolf.* Guilford, Ct.: The Lyons Press, 2005.

Steinhart, Peter. *The Company of Wolves*. New York: Vintage Books/Random House, 1995.

Thayer, Helen. *Three Among Wolves*. Canada: Sasquatch Books, 2004.

Whitt, Chris. *Wolves Life in the Pack.* New York: Main Street/Sterling Publishing Co., 2003.

Printed in the United States
147822LV00001B/2/P

9 781432 736668